**Cart...
man...

MW00423384

yanking the man over onto his back. Holding the Cuban's throat with his left hand, Carter brought the tip of the stiletto up into the man's left nostril.

"Move and I drive the blade into your brain," Carter hissed.

The Cuban was well trained enough to realize that if he moved, if he struggled, he would die instantly.

"Was it Ganin?" Carter snapped.

The Cuban said nothing. There was no reaction to the name in his eyes.

"Arkadi Ganin. Was he in on this operation?" Carter shouted.

"I don't know, señor. I don't know. I swear it."

A vision of Sigourney's face, her smile, her laugh, rose up in Carter's mind. He flicked the stiletto to one side, laying open the man's nose. Blood cascaded over the man's face...

NICK CARTER IS IT!

"Nick Carter out-Bonds James Bond."
—*Buffalo Evening News*

"Nick Carter is America's #1 espionage agent."
—*Variety*

"Nick Carter is razor-sharp suspense."
—*King Features*

"Nick Carter has attracted an army of addicted readers . . . the books are fast, have plenty of action and just the right degree of sex . . . Nick Carter is the American James Bond, suave, sophisticated, a killer with both the ladies and the enemy."
—*New York Times*

FROM THE NICK CARTER
KILLMASTER SERIES

NICK CARTER

KILLMASTER

The Killing Ground

CHARTER BOOKS, NEW YORK

THE KILLING GROUND

A Charter Book/published by arrangement with
The Condé Nast Publications, Inc.

PRINTING HISTORY
Charter edition/January 1986

ISBN: 0-441-57280-4

Charter Books are published by The Berkley Publishing Group.
200 Madison Avenue, New York, New York 10016.
PRINTED IN THE UNITED STATES OF AMERICA

Dedicated to the men of the
Secret Services of the
United States of America

The Killing Ground

PROLOGUE

Wind-driven snow howled around the eaves of the buildings in the vast compound. It was late night, and the temperatures had already plunged well below zero in the Siberian outpost. Far on the other side of the camp, enclosed within a high steel mesh fence, the guards slept in safe isolation. Out in the open, where there were no guards at night, no fences, only the cold weather and thousands of miles of frozen terrain, it was no-man's land. This was a labor camp for some of the worst, most hardened criminals in the Soviet Union. Murderers, rapists, bombers. Russia had them all, though it was never publicized.

A tall, powerfully built man dashed from the corner of one of the buildings into the shadows behind the next. He was oblivious to the cold. His survival that night would depend upon his complete concentration. He could make no mistakes. And to fail would be the biggest mistake of all.

"His name is Balachev. Big man with a scar on his right cheek," the mission-master explained.

"What did he do?"

"He's a nice fellow, let me tell you, Arkadi. He killed his

1

mother, raped and killed both of his sisters, then strangled his
father—who was a steelworker and no small man himself—
after which he cut them all into little pieces and threw them
into the Moscow River. How do you like that?''

''He sounds sick.''

''In camp he's known as 'the enforcer.' Already he's
killed six men.''

''Why hasn't he been taken out of there and shot? Why
play games with someone like that?'' Arkadi Konstantinovich Ganin asked. He and his mission-master sat in a
warm office in the town of Krasnoyarsk.

''He serves two purposes, and so has been too valuable to
execute. He has kept order in the camp. If anyone gets out of
line, he simply kills them.''

''But that has ended?'' There was a hardness to Ganin, but
a natural curiosity, too. He held the KGB rank of colonel.

''Unfortunately yes. We are moving the camp away from
there. The work has been done. There is a new project.
Balachev would be a disruptive element.''

Ganin nodded. He had an idea what might be coming, and
he didn't like it. He was a killer. A highly trained assassin,
the best in the Soviet Union. But like most professionals, he
was not a wanton criminal. When he had a job to do, he did it
with skill and dispatch.

''There was a second reason you mentioned,'' Ganin
prompted.

''Ah, yes, of course, comrade. The second purpose
Balachev will serve will be for your training.''

Ganin sat up. ''What are you saying?''

''Your orders are to go into the camp—tonight—and kill
Comrade Balachev.''

Ganin's dark eyes narrowed. This was stupid. More than
that, it was outrageous.

''Without weapons, Arkadi Konstantinovich. You will be
unarmed.''

"What is the purpose of this assignment?" Ganin asked. His mission-master, whose name he did not know, was a hard man who had trained him well. But he didn't like this at all.

"If you fail, you will be dead, and we will simply shoot poor Balachev in the head to end his misery. If you succeed, you will be assigned to something new out of Moscow. Something that would involve much travel. Overseas travel."

"Yes?"

"It is called Komodel—*Komitet Mokrie Dela*—the State Committee for Wet Affairs."

"There is a Department Viktor in the KGB—" Ganin started, but his mission-master cut him off.

"This is special, Arkadi. This is run by Kobelev himself."

The name Kobelev kept running through Ganin's mind as he studied Barracks A from where he was concealed in the shadows. Atop every fifth building was a strong light that illuminated a wide section of the compound. The one atop the A building flickered intermittently with the wind. Balachev was in that building. Waiting for him. On parting, Ganin's mission-master had informed him that the entire camp knew that someone would be in there to try for the killer. It made the assignment that much more interesting, on Kobelev's orders.

No one would be protecting Balachev; at least Ganin didn't think there would be. But the camp was filled with a thousand pairs of eyes and ears. Balachev would have his watchers. They would be reporting to him on any movement outside.

On the way out to the camp Ganin had devised a dozen plans, scrapping each after a few minutes' reflection. Going up against one man with any kind of stealth would be impossible with all the watchers. In the end it would come down to one thing: a man-to-man fight. One-on-one. Ganin's skill against Balachev's.

Ganin stepped out away from the building behind which he had been crouching and approached the barracks. He could sense that he was being watched. Even the wind died for a moment.

"Balachev!" Ganin shouted. "Vasili Mikhailovich Balachev!"

A light atop the building flickered with a gust of wind, the metal cage over the bulb rattling.

"Balachev!" Ganin shouted again. "You are a motherless whore! A killer of weak people! Come outside and meet your match!"

For several long seconds there was no sound, no movement, and Ganin was about to shout again, when the barracks' door crashed open and a monster of a man burst outside in a blur, bellowing in rage, a long, wicked-looking butcher knife raised over his head.

Ganin was just barely able to feint to the left, then slide right as Balachev charged, the knife swinging in a long, deadly arc, slicing open Ganin's left sleeve.

Suddenly there were hundreds of prisoners pouring out of the barracks, forming a circle in front of the building. Either way the fight went, it would provide entertainment, and some relief. If Balachev won, it would be their blow against the state. If, on the other hand, Ganin should win, it would provide them relief against the monster's tyranny.

Balachev had spun around in the snow, surprisingly light on his feet for his size, and he immediately charged again. This time the knife was in his left hand, and he held it low, so that he could slice upward.

Ganin had only a split second to regain his balance, and he leaped up, kicked out with both feet, catching Balachev square in the chest, and fell back, twisting out of the way as he went down. His movements were hampered by his heavy clothing, however, and he was an instant too late. Balachev buried the knife in the meaty part of Ganin's left thigh, the pain shooting throughout his entire body.

A roar went up from the crowd of prisoners.

Balachev, sensing an early, easy victory, smiled insanely and leaped at the same moment. With superhuman effort, Ganin yanked the knife from his leg, rolled over, and brought it up, stiff-armed, the blade burying itself to the hilt in the big man's chest.

Nikolai Fedor Kobelev stood at the window of his third-floor office looking out across Dzerzhinskogo Plaza toward Lubyanka Prison and the downtown building that headquartered the KGB. His Department Viktor office had been over there at one time. But the place was a madhouse. One hand had no idea what the other was doing. He had often maintained that the KGB's downfall would come not because of Western coups; it would collapse of its own ponderous weight.

"Fools and opportunists, more interested in licking their superiors' boots than doing a creative, intelligent job," he muttered.

A knock came at his door.

"Come in," he snapped.

His secretary Ivan Stanovich came in. "We have gotten word from Krasnoyarsk, Comrade General."

"Yes?" Kobelev barked without turning around.

"Balachev is dead."

"Ganin was successful, then?"

"Yes, Comrade General, although he was wounded."

"Seriously?" Kobelev demanded.

"No, sir. A leg wound. He will be fit for duty very soon."

"Good. I want him here within thirty-six hours."

"Sir," Stanovich snapped, and he departed.

Kobelev went back to his thoughts. Ganin was very good, the best in the Soviet Union at the moment. His little test in Krasnoyarsk would be nothing, however, compared to the real thing that would come very soon. Kobelev could almost taste the sweet victory that would be his when, at long last, like Balachev, Nick Carter, of the ultrasecret American intelligence agency AXE, was buried in the ground, his heart stilled forever.

ONE

The big 747 arriving from Phoenix, Arizona, touched down a few minutes before ten on a cold evening at Washington's National Airport. Nick Carter, a tall, dark-haired, well-built man, limped from the first-class section, through the boarding tunnel, and out into the main terminal. As far as he was concerned, he'd been too long recovering at AXE's rest and rehabilitation facility outside Phoenix. It was time for a change of scenery.

For more years than Carter wanted to count, he had worked for AXE, which, under the guise of Amalgamated Press and Wire Services, was a highly specialized intelligence gathering and special action agency. Anything too tough or dirty for the CIA, the National Security Agency, or the individual military service intelligence establishments was taken on by AXE. And among his peers within AXE, Carter was simply the best. He carried an N3 designation, which meant that when on assignment he was licensed to kill, authorized to carry out what the Soviets called *mokrie dela*, or wet affairs—assassinations.

As he threaded his way through the crush of late-night

7

passengers in the terminal, he walked with a pronounced limp. He had just come off an assignment during which he had very nearly been killed. The bullet had hit low, doing some damage to the thigh bone in his right leg. AXE doctors, who were some of the best anywhere, had taken him apart and put him back together again, as they had so many times before. It would be months before he regained complete use of his leg, but for now, at least he was ambulatory.

Carter was a man unlike other men, in that within him his sense of survival, his sense of self-preservation, was very much stronger than usual. On more than one occasion he had completed his assignment half dead from wounds or exhaustion. Where other men tried and failed, Carter never failed.

At times he was bored during the gaps between assignments. But at other times, such as this moment, he was looking forward to the next thirty days.

Enforced R&R, it was called. Coming off such an assignment as he had, it was required that he rest for a month or so. Once he was released from the hospital, however, there was no real reason for him to remain in Arizona, so he had signed himself out back to Washington, and had returned. But he wasn't planning on staying in town very long.

He took the escalator down to incoming baggage, where a few minutes later he retrieved his two leather suitcases and then swung out to the passenger pick-up area.

His timing was just right. A brown Mercedes 450SL, its convertible top up against the chill fall air, pulled up, and the trunk popped open.

Smiling, Carter tossed his bags in the back, slammed the trunk lid, and climbed in the passenger seat, into the arms of a tall, auburn-haired beauty with large, liquid brown eyes and warm, sensuous lips. They kissed deeply for a long moment, until a cab behind them beeped.

They parted, and Sigourney Veltman looked into Carter's dark eyes. She smiled wanly and shook her head.

"You look like hell, you know," she said. Her voice was soft, gentle, and held an upper-class Connecticut accent.

Carter grinned. "Not exactly the first words I thought I'd hear," he said.

"I'll fix that."

"Promise?"

"Promise," she said, laughing. She put the car in gear and pulled smoothly away from the curb, accelerating down the long ramp and out the main airport exit.

Carter lit one of his custom-blended cigarettes, his initials stamped in gold on the filter, and sat back in the thick, soft leather seat. He had to admit to himself that he was tired. The day before, against doctor's orders, he had taken an exploratory run through AXE's very difficult desert confidence course. His time was one of his slowest ever, and he had been angry with himself. The course master, however, had been amazed.

"Slow my ass, Carter," he had shouted at the end. "An ordinary man would have been dead halfway through. What the hell are you trying to prove?"

"I just want to stay alive the next time, Roger," Carter said.

"Won't be a next time if you keep this up."

Carter and Roger Caldwell went back years. The thick-necked, beefy confidence course instructor had at one time been a crack AXE agent. A particularly difficult and dirty assignment had left him with one arm missing, the bones in both of his legs shattered, and only one kidney. They had taken him off active-duty assignments, but his recovery had been nothing short of miraculous. These days he was a tough man. Carter had a great deal of respect for him.

"Get some rest, soak up some sun, drink a little, and get hold of a sweet-talking woman who won't raise your blood pressure. Then come back in a month and we'll see if you can challenge the course."

"I think I'll do just that," Carter had said. "And I've got the perfect lady in mind to do it with."

Sigourney was the divorced daughter of Karl Stearnes, a special adviser to the President on security matters. Her ex-husband was a West German. He worked as an attaché at the German embassy in Washington. They weren't really meant for each other, and the marriage didn't last long, but they were still friends. The man was now married to a pleasant, down-to-earth Bavarian woman, and they had two children. Sigourney had once told Carter she felt almost like the children's aunt. It was very strange.

On occasion she did contract work for AXE. With her beauty, her poise, and her obvious intelligence she was a natural at any foreign embassy party, where she could easily gather needed information.

She and Carter had met at one of those functions—which he usually hated—and had immediately clashed. She'd be damned if any man was going to tell her what to do.

Months later they were again on an assignment, and this time the sparks flew even more. Somehow, though, by the end of the evening he had ended up at her apartment and they had made passionate, almost violent love. He always supposed she had been trying to prove something to him that night: that she wasn't just some empty-headed, convenient woman to be used simply for adornment.

"A penny," she said, breaking him out of his thoughts.

He looked at her. "I was just thinking back to when we first met."

She laughed out loud. "Oh, boy, what a bastard you were. Couldn't tell you a damned thing. You were king of the walk . . . at least that's how you tried to set yourself up."

"You know, I damned near turned you over my knee right there in front of the Belgian ambassador and spanked you."

"If you had tried, I would have gouged your eyes out," she shot back.

They both laughed again.

"I'm glad you could break free on such short notice," he said softly.

She glanced at him, and reached out and touched his cheek with her fingers. "Weather's been lousy around here lately. Where'd you say it was we were going?"

"St. Anne's Island Resort. It's a tiny private island in the Caribbean. In the Turks and Caicos. We'll have it all to ourselves, and a small staff."

"Sounds nice, Nick," she said, and she glanced again at him, this time with a more critical eye. "You do look like hell. But we've got a month to make you all better."

"Starting tonight?"

She nodded. "I've got most of your things packed, your apartment will be okay, and I've checked on your car, extending the storage contract."

"You really are something. Thanks," Carter said.

"Oh, yes, one last thing," she added. "Hawk called this evening, just before I left for the airport. Said he wanted you to call as soon as you got in."

Carter sat up. David Hawk was the hard-bitten director of AXE. He had been a power in the old days with the OSS, and when AXE was created by special presidential order, he had been the logical choice to head it. During the years Carter had worked for the man, they had developed a relationship of mutual understanding and respect that at times bordered on a father-son intensity, although they rarely verbalized their deep affection.

When David Hawk called, Carter dropped everything and came running. He was the only man in the world who commanded such loyalty in N3.

"Did he say what it was about?"

Sigourney shook her head. "Not really. Just that it wasn't something to worry about . . . for now."

●   ●   ●

They drove the rest of the way to Carter's new Georgetown condo near the university in silence, parked in the back, and walked upstairs.

Inside, the table was set for two, white wine was chilling in a bucket, candles were ready to be lit, and the air was full of the aroma of something being kept warm in the kitchen. Carter remembered that in addition to Sigourney's other attributes, she was an excellent cook.

She fixed him a scotch with one cube, then went into the kitchen while he went to the phone and dialed Hawk's private number, which was answered on the first ring.

"I'm back, sir," Carter said.

"I won't hold you long, Nick. Sigourney tells me you two will be leaving first thing in the morning."

"Yes, sir. But if there's something . . ."

"Nothing to hold you, really. But Caldwell called and said you were pushing yourself. How do you feel?"

Carter's first instinct was to lie. Tell Hawk he felt fit. But no one ever lied to David Hawk. Not for very long, at any rate. And when the lie was caught, the consequences were always swift and not at all good for the liar.

"I've felt better, sir."

"I'll bet. I don't want you pushing yourself again. When you get back, you're going into the hospital for a complete checkup."

"Yes, sir."

Carter could hear Sigourney in the kitchen. She was humming some tune he couldn't recognize.

"Something has come up, Nick, that you should know about," Hawk began. "Nothing we can do anything about at the moment, but I suspect before too long we're going to have some trouble on our hands. So I want you to be on your guard. Don't back yourself into any corners."

Carter held his silence, but he was beginning to get a gut feeling that something very bad was coming down.

"We've just gotten the first bits about something new in Moscow. There's been a split, it seems, within the KGB's hierarchy."

"Sir?"

"Department Viktor—the assassination department within the Komitet—has apparently been shut down. Lock, stock, and barrel."

"That doesn't make any sense," Carter muttered.

"On the surface it doesn't. But we think they've started up something new, something much better. From what we can gather it's called Komodel—short for *Komitet Mokrie Dela*—the State Committee for Wet Affairs—and deals with terrorism and assassination."

Sigourney came from the kitchen and placed a large cast-iron pot on a trivet on the table. It was bouillabaisse; he could smell the seafood and the saffron.

"Who is running it, sir? Who is the brains behind it?"

"That's just it, Nick. We can't find out. It's a highly secret, very closed shop. It was only pure luck that we got any information at all. But we do know one thing."

Carter waited. Sigourney was looking at him, a concerned expression in her wide eyes.

"Arkadi Konstantinovich Ganin is apparently connected with this organization."

Ganin, Nick thought. He was the Soviet Union's very best operative, bar none. A very tough and elusive man. No one who could provide his description had ever lived to pass it out. His existence was known through his terrible deeds. But there were no photographs of him anywhere in the West.

"If Ganin is on the loose, there will be trouble," Carter said.

"You could be a likely target, Nick," Hawk said evenly. "I want you to watch yourself."

"Perhaps I should stick around. We're going to have to go after him."

"No," Hawk said sharply. "Not now. Not yet. There will be time. The first move will be theirs. When it happens, we'll go after them." Hawk hesitated for a moment. "In the meantime I want you to get yourself back in shape. Against Ganin, if it comes to that, you're going to have to be whole. No, *more* than that—you'll need a hundred and *ten* percent."

"Yes, sir."

"If anything comes up, I'll be in contact," Hawk said. "And, Nick?"

"Yes?"

"Have a good vacation."

"Thanks," Carter said, and he hung up. He took a sip of his scotch and stood there for a long moment, deep in thought. Ganin. It was a name to command respect. The name of a man who understood deadly force as if he had invented it.

"Bouillabaisse, anyone?" Sigourney called softly.

Carter turned, and managed a slight smile.

"Should I ask?"

He shook his head. "I'm on vacation, starting now," he said. He tossed back the rest of his drink and came to the table. They would be fairly isolated for the next month. Nothing was going to develop that quickly, and even if it did, they'd be insulated by their distance.

The chill Washington fall seemed a century ago to Nick Carter as their Cayman Airways flight came in on its landing approach to Grand Turk Island in the British West Indies. The intense, multishaded blue water seemed speckled with green jewels of islands in every direction, except due north into the open Atlantic, for as far as the eye could see. From the air it looked like paradise.

His mind was truly at ease for the first time in as long as he could remember. Only the slightest nagging thought lingered about Komodel and Arkadi Ganin, and he suspected that even that errant worry would leave within the next twenty-four hours.

He turned and looked at Sigourney. She wore a silk blouse, a simple wraparound skirt, and sandals. She was watching out the window, as excited as a little girl going to her first party. "Oh, Nick, I'm so happy," she kept saying, squeezing his hand.

Carter smiled. The night before, after her excellent dinner, they had taken a long, hot, leisurely bath together, and then she had literally put him to bed, he had become so weak, so limp.

"Big tough operative, huh?" she had chided him.

He remembered that he was hardly able to keep his eyes open, let alone reach up for her. The last thing he remembered was her body next to his, holding him tight, cooing in his ear to sleep, to let go, to relax and drift off. Which is what he had done.

In the morning he was still sore and bone-weary, but he felt better than he had for a long time.

Sigourney turned away from the window as the 727's wheels hit the runway, and the big aircraft lurched as the brakes were applied.

"An entire month?" she said.

Carter had to laugh out loud. "An entire month in which neither of us has to share the other with anyone."

She pursed her lips, her nose wrinkling. "I just hope I don't get bored. One man? . . . Just one?"

"You have a round-trip ticket," he said solemnly, his eyes twinkling.

She reached over and hugged his arm. "I may never want to go back, Nick," she said.

Customs was simple, and within a few minutes after landing, they took a cab down to the quay and found the boat that would ferry them across to tiny St. Anne's Island. The weather was absolutely lovely: temperature in the low eighties, a soft trade wind from the east, and puffy white clouds sailing overhead at their own leisurely pace.

St. Anne's was seventeen miles away, down toward Salt Cay, and the run in the forty-two-foot luxury cruiser operated by the resort took less than two hours. The island was almost perfectly round, with a fifty-foot hill in the center of its ten acres. The beaches were stunningly white, the cottages quaint and spotlessly clean, and the main house was just large enough to be comfortable without losing its Caribbean ambience.

In addition to two groundsmen, the staff included two maids, a houseman, two cooks, and a maintenance man-cum-scuba instructor.

They introduced themselves, helped Carter and Sigourney unpack, and then left.

"If there is anything . . . anything you need, just call, we'll be there," Arthur, the houseman, said in his lilting Caribbean accent.

It was very late afternoon, and the sun was sinking into the western sea. Sigourney stepped out onto the patio, which was barely fifty feet from the pure white beach, and shuddered with pleasure. She turned.

"This island is ours? Exclusively?"

"Except for the staff."

"Who are discreet."

"Who are discreet," Carter agreed.

"Pour the champagne," she said, undoing her skirt and letting it fall. "I want to make up for last night."

Carter opened the champagne chilling on the sideboard as Sigourney took off her blouse and bra, then stepped out of her bikini panties. She was a beautiful woman, her breasts proud and firm, her nipples pink. Her belly was only slightly rounded, and her legs were long, straight, and beautifully formed, beginning at a soft swatch of dark hair.

She turned suddenly and ran down to the beach, plunging

into the surf as Carter got undressed, then brought the champagne down to the sand.

"Nick . . . oh, Nick!" she cried from the water, a wave crashing over her.

He went back up to the house, got a large beach towel, and brought it back, spreading it out on the white sand.

"Come on in!" Sigourney called, splashing. "My God, it's great!"

Carter marched down into the surf as another wave broke over Sigourney, knocking her flat. He helped her up, and she started to say something, when she suddenly stopped.

"Nick . . . ?" she breathed.

Carter pulled her to him, her breasts crushed against his chest, her legs against his, and kissed her hard, her tongue suddenly darting into his mouth.

When they parted, her skin was flushed. She was smiling, her nostrils flared, her eyes wide, her lips moist. "I love you," she said.

Carter picked her up, carried her back to the beach, and set her down gently on the large towel. She was limp in his arms, her eyes moist.

"I love you . . ." she murmured weakly as Carter kissed her left breast, and then her right, his tongue lingering on her nipples, around the areola, then encircling the entire breast.

She moaned. Her knees came up.

Carter kissed the area between her breasts, then ran his tongue down to her belly button, where he again lingered, her hips rising to meet his touch.

She was shivering now, not from the wind, because it was warm, but because of her passion. Her entire body thrummed like the plucked string of a violin.

Her thighs were wonderfully smooth as Carter worked his way up from behind her knees.

She reached down and took his head in her hands. "Nick!" she cried. "I want you now!"

He came into her deeply, slowly at first, her pelvis rising sharply to meet his, her body shuddering, her eyes closed but her mouth half open, a golden glow radiating from her skin.

Slowly, gently, purposefully he pulled away, and then thrust deeper so that it seemed as if her entire body would envelop his, so that they were one vibration together, one instrument being played in unison, singing out their passion.

Forgotten were past hurts and injuries; forgotten were Hawk's warnings, and the previous night's tiredness; forgotten was everything but the ecstatic moment.

"Nick . . . oh, Nick, I love you," Sigourney cried softly as their lovemaking seemed to go on and on forever, and they both seemed to balance on the very peak of a tall, wonderful mountain before plunging together into sensual oblivion.

Just as Carter opened his eyes and looked down at her, she opened hers.

"I do love you," she said.

"And I think I love you," he replied.

TWO

Arkadi Ganin stepped out of the diplomatic exit of the United Nations Building, nodded to the security guard as he passed, then walked the few blocks up 42nd Street to the Grand Hyatt Hotel.

It was raining and blustery, but heedless of the weather, Ganin reviewed in his mind the preparations he had completed here in New York, and elsewhere. The plan that Kobelev had worked out in painstaking detail was as bold and dangerous as it was faultlessly brilliant.

Ganin had been on a lot of assignments in his distinguished career, but none could ever compare to this one. It was the sort of thing he liked most. This time there would be no flabby, unaware politician for him to kill, no military leader, no general, no diplomat. This time he was going after a much more interesting target. A target that certainly could and most assuredly would fight back. It would come to a one-on-one fight.

At the luxury hotel next to Grand Central Station, he took the elevator up to his twelfth-floor room and finished packing the rest of his things in his black leather Gucci suitcase and carry-on bag.

The Western world, he felt, for all its supposed openness and freedom, was like a fast-running horse with blinders on. People saw what they wanted to see. A man such as Arkadi, traveling under the name Bruno Hildebrandt, a wealthy West German businessman who dressed well and carried expensive luggage, could not be a Soviet operative. Soviet operatives were shambling, ugly monsters who wore baggy suits.

He glanced at his gold Rolex, and grinned. "Stupid bastards," he mumbled. He went to the window that looked down on 42nd Street, noting its traffic and its clogged sidewalks. There was no order here. No organization. Everything seemed to be in chaos. This was nothing, however, to the chaos he was going to wreak on a certain member of the American intelligence community.

After checking to make sure he hadn't forgotten anything, Ganin left a tip for the maid, then took his bags downstairs, where he checked out, paying for his stay with his American Express card. Outside, he got a cab and ordered the driver to take him out to Kennedy, then he settled back with his thoughts for the long ride.

Nikolai Kobelev was a man of great power and intelligence who nevertheless had one fault: his all-consuming hatred for the AXE Killmaster, Nick Carter. Ganin wasn't sure of all the details, but he knew it had something to do with Kobelev's daughter, now dead, and some series of operations in which Kobelev himself had very nearly been killed.

There was an obsessive, almost blind rage in the new master of Komodel that would not go away until Carter was killed. It was dangerous, but Ganin, who had languished in a lot of petty little assignments recently, was glad for the challenge.

"I want him dead, Arkadi," Kobelev had said, pacing in his office in Moscow. "But first I want him to suffer, as I have. I want him to feel the same losses I have felt. I want him to understand that nothing he can do will alter the outcome. I want him to know real fear.''

Ganin was seated across the desk from Kobelev, the wound in his thigh throbbing. There was a metal plate, silver and shiny, covering much of the back of Kobelev's head.

"In the end he will beg us to kill him, Arkadi. He will beg us, this you must understand.''

Ganin nodded.

Kobelev stopped his pacing and leaned over his desk, his dark eyes boring into Ganin's.

"There will be no mistakes. Your own life will depend upon it. Do you understand that as well?''

Again Ganin nodded. "It will be as you ask, Comrade General. There will be no escape for Carter. In the end he will be glad of his death.''

Kobelev straightened up and rubbed his hands together. "Oh, yes,'' he said, smiling, his eyes bright. "Oh, yes, I am going to enjoy this very much.''

Preparations in Moscow had taken only forty-eight hours. A further five days in Western Europe completed the arrangements there, and Ganin had flown the day before to New York City to complete the last of the business.

The opening move, according to Kobelev's plan, would come as suddenly as lightning. "A bolt from out of the heavens!''

Ganin was in time for his flight down to Washington, D.C., where he connected with the 12:45 P.M. Cubana Airlines flight direct to Havana, Cuba. The plane was a Tupolev TU-154, filled to capacity mostly with wild-looking Cuban characters on their way home from some sort of a function in Washington. All the way down they drank and argued and screamed their notions of the people's revolution.

Ganin thought his fellow passengers ridiculous and annoying. He kept to himself as much as he could, but by the time they landed in Havana and went through the customs check, he was in a foul mood.

A staff car from the Soviet embassy was waiting for him outside the airport terminal. He threw his bags in the front seat and climbed in the back. The KGB's Havana *resident*, Viktor Chalkin, sat in the corner, a worried expression on his face.

"Arkadi Konstantinovich," he said softly.

They shook hands. "You're looking well, Viktor," Ganin said.

The driver got in, and they headed into the city, the glass partition between the front and back seats giving them soundproof privacy.

"You had a pleasant flight down, I trust," the KGB man said. He and Ganin had worked together out of Lisbon some years back. Ganin had respect for the man, but he had heard that Chalkin had been hitting the bottle pretty heavily. There had been talk about his recall from Havana, a move that would sound the death knell for his career.

"Absolutely rotten. Goddamned revolutionaries and their prattle."

Chalkin laughed. "You ought to be living down here with them. It's a wonder they ever could have mounted a revolution, let alone win it."

They rode in silence for a few minutes, until Ganin glanced over at his old comrade.

"I didn't come this way for small talk about the Cuban mentality."

"No," Chalkin said. "I understand that, Arkadi."

"The preparations have been made?"

Chalkin nodded heavily. "In fact two of the rabble who came down on the plane with you will be assigned to the team." He shook his head. He looked like a trapped man. "Arkadi, this will create a lot of trouble just when things were beginning to settle down."

"You don't know the trouble," Ganin said. "But it will be done. You can't imagine the trouble if we fail."

"I know. They say he's . . . crazy."

"Don't ever say that!" Ganin shouted. "Unless you want to be put up against a wall and shot! He'd do it himself!"

Chalkin seemed to gather himself up. "Right," he said. "Tonight or tomorrow night, your choice, Arkadi."

Ganin looked out at the landscape they were passing. Palm trees waved in the gentle tropical breezes. Peace, of a sort, had come to this island. It wouldn't last long, though. Nothing ever lasted long. He turned back to Chalkin.

"Tonight," he said.

Chalkin nodded. "The helicopter is ready. We'll have you and your team over the drop zone no later than one in the morning. From there you should make it ashore by two, do your business, and get the hell out of there within an hour. The chopper will be back over the pickup point at three A.M. But it won't stay for more than five minutes, so your timing will have to be tight. All that without practice."

"It'll work out," Ganin said. "The men all understand the target?"

"Yes, they do, Arkadi."

The night was almost unbelievably beautiful. Ten billion stars seemed to have been flung on a velvet backdrop from horizon to horizon, lending a fairy-tale atmosphere to an already enchanted scene.

Nick Carter could not remember the last time he had felt so good, so relaxed, so at ease. The ten days he and Sigourney had been on St. Anne's had gone by in a flash. But they had twenty more glorious days left. He had been sure that after this long, he would have begun to get bored. But it hadn't happened that way. Not with her.

He was seated alone on the broad veranda of the main house. They had finished dinner a little while ago, and Sigourney had gone inside to fetch them some brandy and coffee while he smoked a cigarette.

His leg was much better, the headaches had gone, and Carter was rested; he was fit. Not Hawk's 110 percent, perhaps, but getting there.

He sighed deeply and sat back.

"Oh, my, that sounded positively lazy," Sigourney called from the door. She came out onto the veranda with a tray that she set down on the wicker table. She came to him, snuggling into his lap, and kissed his ear.

"Bored yet?" she asked at length.

"No. You?"

"I never want to go back," she answered. "I have everything I want or need right here."

They both wore shorts, she wore one of his T-shirts, and he was bare-chested. She intertwined her fingers in the hair on his chest, then bent down and kissed his nipples.

Carter laughed. "The coffee will get cold," he said.

"Screw the coffee," Sigourney replied breathlessly. She got up, took his hands in hers, and started to pull him up when the marine telephone in the back beeped twice.

They both looked toward the door. The phone, which was hooked via single-sideband radio to the main island, beeped again.

"Damn," Sigourney swore.

"Is Arthur inside?" Carter asked.

"He's with Maria," Sigourney said. "I told all of them to take the rest of the night off."

The phone beeped a third time, and Carter got to his feet and went inside. He flipped the switch on the console and picked up the handset. There was only one person who would be calling him here.

"Yes?" he said, his heartbeat quickening.

"Nick, I'm sorry to bother you like this," David Hawk, his voice distorted by the SSB transmission, said over the line.

"It's all right, sir," Carter said. "Is there a problem?"

"There might be, Nick. We're just not sure. But I figured I'd better let you know."

"Yes, sir."

"Remember our conversation about a certain friend from the other side. An expert?"

Hawk meant Ganin, of course. "Yes, sir, I remember. Is there more news?"

"Perhaps. Our people in Havana seem to think he's there. In Cuba. Right at this moment."

On assignment? Carter asked himself. To do what?

"He is very close to you, Nick. A couple of hundred miles. I thought you'd better know. Just be a little careful."

"Yes, sir," Carter said, his mind racing. "Thanks for calling me."

"Are you . . . all right? How do you feel?"

"Never felt better, sir," Carter said. "Never felt better."

"I'm glad to hear it, Nick. When you get back we'll have to do something about our mutual friend. He makes me nervous being this close."

"I thought no one knew what he looked like," Carter said.

"He wasn't actually seen. One of the Company boys working in the Soviet embassy overheard mention that he was there. That's it. Nothing more substantial than that to go on."

An alarm bell rang in Carter's head. It was a mistake, perhaps? But Ganin was a man with the reputation of never making a mistake. Or was there something else to it?

"Thank you again, sir. We'll be on our guard here."

"Say hello to Sigourney for me, and enjoy the rest of your vacation," Hawk said, and he clicked off.

Carter put down the handset and flipped the switch. He turned. Sigourney had come to the door. She was looking at him.

"Trouble?" she asked.

"I don't know," Carter said. Quickly he told her what Hawk had said. When he was finished she shivered.

"Do you think he'll come here? Could he know you're here?"

"I don't know, Sigourney. I just don't know. But it's damned coincidental that he'd be in Cuba the same time as we're here."

"What are you going to do, Nick?"

"Nothing much," he said. "We'll just keep our eyes and ears open. I'll talk to the staff in the morning. If anyone approaches the island, they can sound the alarm. We'll be all right."

Sigourney was silent for several long seconds, but then she beckoned. "There's some unfinished business out here," she said, smiling.

"I'll be right there," Carter said, and abruptly he turned and went into the back bedroom where his suitcase with his street clothes and other things was stored.

She followed him inside and stood at the doorway as he opened the suitcase and pulled out his weapons, checking each to make sure it was ready for instant action should the need arise.

Wilhelmina, his perfectly balanced 9mm Luger. Hugo, his thin, razor-sharp stiletto in its chamois sheath. And Pierre, an AXE-designed gas bomb, about the size of a large marble, that could permanently incapacitate a room filled with people within seconds. Old friends, all of them. Companions who never failed him and who had saved his life on countless occasions. But old friends, nevertheless, that were and would continue to be well bloodied.

Carter levered a round into the Luger's firing chamber, made sure the safety was on, and stuffed the weapon into the waistband of his shorts.

"Let's go for a little walk," he said, taking Sigourney's hand and leading her outside to the veranda and then down the short path to the beach.

Away from the house they could see the glow of the lights from the town on the big island. There was only a light breeze, the tiny wavelets lapping softly on the white beach. Something jumped out in the water.

"Should I be frightened, Nick?" Sigourney asked, her voice hushed.

Carter looked at her and smiled. "I don't think so. We'll watch what's happening, but I don't think there's really anything to worry about."

For a long time they stared out across the water. Then Sigourney shrugged. "The coffee by now is certainly cold," she said.

"Screw the coffee," Carter replied, and laughing, they went hand in hand back to the house.

It was after eleven o'clock. The night was very warm and humid. The steady chop of the slowly spinning rotors of the big Sikorsky helicopter warming up on the pad was nearly deafening.

Seven men, all of them dressed in black, their faces and hands darkened, stood in a rigid line at attention. Each carried a small but heavy pack that contained explosives as well as their own personal ammunition. Uzi submachine guns were slung over their shoulders. Chalkin thought using the Israeli weapon was somehow a fitting touch.

The embassy limousine pulled up, and Ganin, also dressed in black and carrying a bag and an Uzi, jumped out. A moment later Chalkin followed.

"The pilot has his orders," Chalkin was saying. "They've all been briefed. Nothing should go wrong."

"I don't suspect it will, Viktor," Ganin said, a hard edge to his voice. In the middle of an assignment he never had time for chatter.

He strode across the tarmac toward the waiting helicopter where the seven men were lined up. One by one he inspected them, their weapons, and their kits, making sure everything was in order. When he was finished he stepped back.

"You all understand your orders?" he shouted in Spanish. Ganin was fluent in ten languages.

"*Si, señor*," all seven replied in unison.

Chalkin had come up from the car. Ganin turned to him.

"They are ready?" the KGB *rezident* asked.

Ganin nodded. Another car had come onto the tarmac. Ganin glanced toward it. "What is his name?"

"Ortega," Chalkin said, following his gaze. "He works in Translation."

"You're sure he's the one?"

"Absolutely. He was set up. There is no doubt he heard that you were coming."

"He passed on the word?"

"His case officer is Charles Knell. We photographed their meeting."

"But you didn't interfere with it?"

"No, Arkadi, of that you have my complete assurance. Ortega knew you were coming, he passed on the information to his case officer, and then he returned to us."

"What has he been told about tonight?"

"He understands he was to come here to help interrogate a few Mexicans. That's all," Chalkin said. He waved toward the car.

"Fine," Ganin said.

"But, Arkadi, I think it is a very dangerous thing to have brought him here. He may see you, provide a description. We cannot be sure he won't slip away from us."

Ganin smiled grimly. "Oh, yes, we *can* be sure, Viktor. Very sure." Ganin reached inside his black jump suit, withdrew a 9mm Beretta automatic, and concealing it at his side, he quickly strode across the parking ramp to where the car was waiting.

Viktor Chalkin started after him but then thought better of it. The seven troops remained stiffly at attention.

At the car Ganin tapped on the opaque window, which was powered down. A man of about thirty-five, his eyes wide, looked out.

"We know about Charles Knell," Ganin said, and he raised the Beretta and fired two shots in quick order, the first catching Ortega in the face just to the right of his nose, and the second blowing the top of the man's forehead off, blood, bits of bone, and white matter flying across the inside of the car, Ortega's body driven back against the opposite door.

Ganin made sure the Beretta's safety was on, holstered the weapon, then searched for and found the two spent shell casings, which he pocketed.

He went back to Chalkin, who had paled.

"I want his body held until three o'clock, and then I want it flown down to the U.S. naval station at Guantánamo Bay, where I want it dumped on their doorstep."

Chalkin swallowed hard.

"Do you understand my simple instructions, Viktor?"

Chalkin nodded. "There will be a lot of trouble over this, Arkadi."

"Yes, there will be," Ganin agreed. "Perhaps we will have some vodka together when I return in the morning. That would be nice."

Again Chalkin swallowed hard and nodded.

Ganin motioned for the troops to board the helicopter, and when they were safely strapped in, he climbed up with the pilot and copilot and gave them the thumbs-up sign to take off.

The big helicopter shuddered, then rose up into the night sky, countless stars twinkling overhead, the lights of the airport and Havana spread along the coast below, and the dark Caribbean Sea toward Florida to the north.

Ganin had donned a helmet with built-in headset and microphone. The copilot showed him where it plugged in, and suddenly he could hear the Havana control tower operators chattering. They were a commercial flight, supposedly on their way down to Santiago de Cuba, the major city on the far southeastern end of the island.

From there, they would drop down to within fifty feet of the water and head across to Great Inagua Island, staying well north of Matthew Town.

That was the halfway point; if they had not been detected by then, if there were no stray U.S. naval vessels around, they would continue. Ganin could almost smell the start of the hunt. Carter would never know what hit him.

"I want you to be close enough to see his face, Arkadi Konstantinovich," Kobelev had instructed him. "I want you to be able to tell me exactly what it was you saw in his eyes."

THREE

Something had awakened Carter. He raised his left arm so that he could see his watch. It was just about two o'clock. The moon had set earlier; now only the light from the stars provided any illumination through the open windows. A light breeze ruffled the curtains, and he could just make out the gentle lapping of the waves on the beach below the house.

"What is it?" Sigourney asked from beside him.

"Did I wake you?"

"No," she said. "I thought I heard something. But I'm just jumpy."

Carter sat up, his hand reaching for Wilhelmina on the night table. "What did you hear?"

"Nothing . . ." she started, but then she sat up. "Hear it?" she asked softly.

He had indeed. And he thought he knew what it was. Carter jumped out of the bed, fingered the Luger's safety to the off position, and stepped over to the window. He kept well within the shadows so that he provided less of a target from outside.

His eyes scanned the area along the beach, and a few yards

31

offshore, but he couldn't make out a thing. The noise he thought he heard had sounded very much like a pair of oars dipping into the water.

He stood there by the window for a full five minutes, but there were no further sounds, nor was anything moving below. Yet Hawk's telephone warning was there. It nagged at him. Some visceral feeling deep in his gut was warning him.

"Anything?" Sigourney asked softly from the bed. The sheet covering her had fallen away, exposing her lovely breasts. Her dark hair was down around her shoulders.

"Get dressed," Carter whispered. He went around to the bureau along the far wall, got a pair of shorts, and pulled them on as Sigourney was pulling on her shorts and top. He stuffed his sheathed stiletto into the waistband of his shorts, transferred Wilhelmina to his left hand, and picked up Pierre, the deadly gas bomb, with his right. The dull metal casing gleamed in the soft light.

He turned as Sigourney was finishing, then went to her. "Here," he said, handing her the device.

She looked into his eyes, then took the gas bomb.

"I want you to stay here, in this room, no matter what happens," he said.

She nodded.

"We may be having some company," he said. He glanced toward the window. "I'm going out."

Her eyes widened and her nostrils flared. "Ganin?" she asked.

"Possibly," Carter said. "Now, listen to me, Sigourney." He quickly explained exactly what Pierre was and how it worked. "If anyone comes in, twist the case, toss it, and hold your breath. This new gas is active for less than thirty seconds. But during that time it's extremely deadly."

Sigourney swallowed hard, but she nodded her understanding. "Be careful, Nick," she said, and hugged him fiercely.

He kissed her. "Be right back," he said. He turned and slipped out of the bedroom, across the darkened living room, and out the back way.

If Ganin was involved with the new KGB assassination department, one of his first targets might likely be Carter. Hawk was worried about it, otherwise he would not have called him. With Ganin less than two hundred miles away in Cuba, the call was justified. On the other hand, Carter thought, it was possible they were overreacting. There was no real reason at this particular moment to think Ganin would be after him. Still, the coincidental arrival of the KGB's master assassin so close was something to think about.

Keeping low, and well in the shadows, Carter crossed behind the house, off the path, and into the thick brush and palmettos that led down to the staff quarters a couple of hundred yards away.

He stopped every few yards to scan the beach and listen for sounds. But there was nothing. One part of him was beginning to feel a bit foolish sneaking around out there, with Sigourney back at the house worried. Yet another, more instinctual, part of him was totally alert, his every sense open for the reception of the smallest sound or movement.

The broad path from the main house swung left, merging with the open area around the four small cottages occupied by the resort island's staff. No lights shone from any of the cottages, nor had Carter expected to see any. The staff would all be asleep at this hour.

He had emerged from the brush and was starting across behind the cottages, when a tremendous explosion from the other side of the tiny island shattered the night's silence and lit up the sky.

Carter spun around and looked back the way he had come. For a split second he debated returning for Sigourney, but she was capable, and she had the gas bomb. Instead, he raced toward the path that led up the hill, on the other side of which was the generator shed where he expected the explosion had been set.

Automatic weapons fire sounded from the west, by the boat dock, and as Carter raced toward the crest of the hill he began to feel the first nagging doubts that he may have been set up. The explosion could very well have been a diversion. But for what? To trap him?

Some inner voice reached his consciousness just as he crested the hill, and he rolled left, diving behind a half-dozen palm trees at the same moment as the dry rattle of automatic weapons fire raked the broad path.

He scrambled around the thick bole of one of the trees and stood up as more automatic fire came from below. This time he was able to pinpoint the direction, and in the dim light he could just make out a rubber raft tied up at the dock and two figures racing away from the furiously burning remnants of the generator shed just below him.

Steadying his gun hand against the tree, he squeezed off three shots in rapid succession, the first knocking down the lead figure, the second missing but the third finding its mark, downing the second black-suited attacker.

For several long seconds, Carter remained where he was, in the protection of the hilltop copse, watching for any further movement from below.

Satisfied that the two he had downed would remain down, he raced up over the path and down the hill around the west side of the generator shed.

Reaching the bodies, he scanned the beach area, the dock, and the crest of the hill behind him for any others. A voice at the back of his head was nagging that this had all been too easy. It was some kind of a setup.

He turned the first man over and pulled back the black hood covering his face. A large hole was blown in his chest from Carter's shot. In the light from the burning generator shed, Carter could see that the dead man was a Latino. Quite possibly a Cuban. The same was true of the second man.

Carter stood up. If they were Cubans, and if Ganin had indeed been spotted in Cuba, he could very well be on the island or had at least mounted this operation.

But there was something else. He could feel it thick in the air.

He raced down to the boat dock to see where the black rubber raft was tied. The resort's boat used for diving, formerly moored on the other side of the dock, was settling slowly to the bottom. They had been at it. Carter pulled out Hugo and punctured the rubber raft's four air chambers, which deflated with explosive bangs, then he cut the raft's fabric into irreparable shreds.

If there was anyone else on the island, anyone who was depending upon this means of escape, they would be cut off.

He turned and started back up the hill. Just at that moment, four explosions came one after the other from the other side of the island, accompanied seconds later by a lot of automatic weapons fire.

It *had* been a setup! he thought angrily. The action on his side of the island had been a diversion.

"Sigourney!" Carter shouted into the night, redoubling his efforts, his legs driving like pistons up over the hill and headlong down the other side.

All the staff cottages were on fire, as was the main house. Now, in the light from the flames, Carter could see several men scrambling into rubber rafts pulled up on the beach.

As he ran he snapped off several shots, downing at least one of the men. Two of the others turned and laid down a curtain of automatic weapons fire up the hill toward Carter, pinning him down.

The two rafts were off the beach and into the water, and the black-suited figures were clambering aboard, outboard motors popping to life.

Carter jumped up and snapped off another shot, then raced down the hill as the rubber boats disappeared into the dark night.

He angled away from the staff cottages directly toward the main house, the front wall of which had been blown outward by the force of an explosion.

Fifty yards away from the house, Carter had to pull up short as its roof collapsed in a wall of flames and sparks that shot a hundred feet up into the night sky.

"Sigourney!" he shouted again.

A dark figure raced around from the far side of the house, his form silhouetted in the flames. It stopped, raised something, and Carter just managed to hit the ground as the distinctive rattle of an Uzi submachine gun sounded, the slugs kicking up the sand all around Carter. Then the figure disappeared in the trees toward the other side of the island. Toward the rubber raft. . . .

Carter leaped up and tried to get closer to the burning house, but the heat was too intense. For a long second or two he stood there, his gun held limply in his right hand. If Sigourney was inside, she was dead. There would be no saving her. It was possible, he told himself, that she had gotten out. But deep in his heart, he knew it wasn't so.

A terrible dark rage rose up inside Carter's breast, all but blinding him to one thought: revenge. Still on the island was one of the attackers. One man remained.

Carter thumbed the Luger's safety to the on position, stuffed the weapon into the waistband of his shorts, and with a terrible glint in his eyes withdrew Hugo, his pencil-thin, lethal stiletto.

He turned and once again raced up the hill, dropping low at the crest.

The dark-suited figure was just coming around the tip of the island along the beach. He had not yet reached the boat dock when Carter hurried down the hill, past the still-burning generator shed, past the two bodies, and then into the water.

Holding the knife in his teeth, Carter silently swam directly across to the dock where the dive boat had been sunk and where the shreds of the rubber raft floated around the pilings.

In the darkness, his head just above the water, Carter waited patiently for the hooded figure to come up the beach to the rubber raft. The man stopped every few yards or so to look over his shoulder, then look up toward the crest of the hill as if he were expecting his friends to show up.

He was about thirty feet away from the dock when he spotted the wrecked remains of the rubber raft. He stopped, then stepped back a pace, looking around wildly, his Uzi up and at the ready.

A moment later he spotted the two other dark-suited figures lying off toward the generator shed, and he stumbled as he backed up another pace or two.

It was clear he was frightened now. He knew that he was cut off. He knew that the others had left, and he knew that Carter was somewhere on the island. Alive.

Keeping to the nearly pitch-black darkness beneath the dock, Carter moved closer in toward the beach, his eyes never leaving the man on shore. Two visions kept flashing in his mind: the first of Sigourney in the bedroom as he had left her; the second, the furiously burning main house, the flames leaping high into the night sky. It took everything within himself to maintain control.

The attacker stepped away from the water's edge, hesitated a moment longer, then turned and trotted back along the beach.

Making absolutely no noise, Carter swam to the beach and carefully eased himself out of the water.

The Cuban, now thirty yards away, glanced over his shoulder. Carter dropped flat and froze, and a second later the black-hooded figure continued.

Carter jumped up, and keeping low, the stiletto gripped loosely in his right hand, he raced at full speed toward the retreating figure.

At the last moment, the Cuban, either hearing something or sensing Carter's presence behind him, started to run. But it was too late. Carter leaped onto the man's back, driving him forward and down, the air whooshing out of his lungs.

Carter ripped the Uzi out of the man's grip, tossed it aside, then yanked the man over onto his back. Holding the Cuban's throat with his left hand, he brought the tip of the stiletto up into the man's left nostril.

"Move and I drive the blade into your brain," Carter hissed in perfect Spanish.

The Cuban was well trained enough to realize that if he moved, if he struggled, he would die instantly. His body went slack, his eyes wide, his jaw tight, his lips compressed.

"Was it Ganin?" Carter snapped.

The Cuban said nothing. There was no reaction to the name in his eyes.

"Arkadi Ganin. Was he in on this operation?" Carter shouted.

"I don't know, señor. I don't know. I swear it."

"Who was leading you? Whose operation was this, you bastard?"

"It was the German. Hildebrandt. Colonel Hildebrandt. He came to . . . Havana. He and the Russian."

"What Russian?"

"Chalkin. Viktor Chalkin. He is the KGB in Havana. It was he and the German. They planned this operation."

Carter had heard the name Chalkin. At one time the man had been a fairly good operative working out of East Germany. But the other one. The German. Was it Ganin operating under an alias?

"Did Chalkin and the German come with you—here—tonight?"

"Only the German. He was in charge."

"Who did the German work for?" Carter asked.

The question, surprisingly, produced a reaction in the Cuban. Carter could read faces very well. Saw the slightest tic. The man knew something.

Carter tightened his grip on the Cuban's throat and eased the stiletto a millimeter farther up his nose. A slight trickle of blood rolled down the man's cheek.

"Who did this German work for?" Carter repeated the question. "Where did he get his orders?"

"I don't know . . . I swear!"

"You're lying, and you will die!"

"No . . . no, señor, please!"

A vision of Sigourney's face, her smile, her laugh, rose up in Carter's mind. He flicked the stiletto to one side, laying open the man's nose. Blood cascaded over the man's face, gushing into his eyes and mouth.

"No!" the Cuban screamed.

"Who did the German work for, you son of a bitch!" Carter shouted.

The Cuban was struggling wildly. With great effort Carter held the man still and placed the stiletto blade a fraction of an inch above his left eye.

"New York . . ." the Cuban babbled through bloody lips.

"What about New York?"

"New York . . . New York, the U.N. . . . I swear to Christ . . . Mother of God . . . New York, the U.N. . . ."

"Who at the U.N.?" Carter demanded.

"Lashkin!" the Cuban screamed. Suddenly he had a pistol in his left hand, bringing it around, the hammer cocked, his finger on the trigger, a wild look in his blood-covered eyes.

"Lashkin!" the Cuban screamed again.

At that moment Carter buried the stiletto to its hilt in the man's eye socket, the tip of the blade grating on the bone for a moment, but then penetrating deep into the brain.

The Cuban gave a mighty heave, shuddered violently as if he were having an epileptic fit, and then slumped back, dead.

Carter withdrew his stiletto and rolled back off the body. He flopped down on his back, his eyes open, staring up at the same stars he and Sigourney had made love under just hours earlier.

He had made the one mistake fatal to any field operative: he had fallen in love. He had become vulnerable. He had presented a weak side to his enemies.

''Lashkin.'' He repeated the name out loud. ''The United Nations in New York City. Lashkin.''

Everyone on the island was dead except Carter. By first light he had made sure there were no survivors. Shortly after seven he found what he took to be the charred remains of Sigourney's body in the bedroom of the main house. He had pulled up the mattress where it had been shoved by the force of the explosion, and she had been there, the gas bomb still clutched in her left hand. She had never had the chance to use it.

His head swimming, his stomach churning, pure, raw, venomous hate rising up inside of him, Carter stumbled outside and down to the water's edge, where he stared out across the sea toward the main island a scant seventeen miles distant. Why hadn't someone seen something over there? The explosions and fire had to have been visible for miles. Why had no one come?

There was nothing left of the generator, or of the radio in the main house. He was cut off.

For an hour or so Carter toyed with the idea of attempting to raise the dive boat hull, but he gave it up after diving down to it and inspecting the damage. The attack force had been efficient. They had cut or blasted a hole in the hull fully three feet in diameter.

By three that afternoon, however, he had found his means of escape. The staff, on their off-duty hours, had enjoyed boating and diving. Carter went searching on that side of the island and discovered a small catamaran, its sails intact, that the attacking party had missed.

By four he had the boat rigged and ready to go.

Before he left he walked back up to the main house, but he could not bring himself to go inside where Sigourney's body still lay among the charred timbers. When he got back, AXE would send a team down here; they'd take care of the remains. He supposed, when this was all over, he'd have to talk to her parents. He had met them at some party in Washington. He remembered her mother as a good-looking, classy woman. He did not look forward to facing her. He felt responsible for Sigourney's death.

But that was later.

The weather had been closing in all day, but mindless of the storm clouds gathering to the northeast along the trade-wind belt, and mindless of the rising breeze, Carter raised the cat's sails and shoved the flimsy boat out past the surf line, scrambling aboard and hauling in the sheets.

The boat took off like a rocket, skipping high across the waves, the windward pontoon on which he was perched rising out of the water, a wide wake hissing behind him.

Spray was flying everywhere as Carter pushed the tiny boat to its absolute limits in the rising winds, but he kept seeing Sigourney's face. He kept seeing her body, feeling it next to his; he kept hearing her calling to him, excited about one thing or another. Of all the women he had ever known, she had come most nearly to his idea of a perfect companion, a perfect lover, a perfect mate.

As he sailed he kept searching his memory, kept looking for the mistakes he had made, trying to catalogue the people who knew about their relationship.

There was no doubt in his mind now that Ganin was after

him, and that the opening blow had been Sigourney's life. This Lashkin in New York was only another step in some long, complex plan that would sooner or later pit the Soviet master assassin against Carter.

They had never planned on killing him on the island. Ganin had simply been toying with him. Taking his measure.

But the confrontation would come. Of that Carter was certain, and as he sailed, his lips curled into a cruel smile, a smile totally devoid of any humor, of any warmth.

When the time came, Carter decided, he would enjoy very much witnessing Ganin's death. His very slow, very painful death.

The only thing that bothered him at that moment was why the Soviets were going to these lengths. They could have killed him on the island. Why had they given him a chance? Why were they toying with him?

Whatever the reason, when it was done, Carter swore, Ganin and whoever ran him would rue the day they had conceived their evil plan.

FOUR

A car and driver were waiting for Carter at Washington's National Airport. His weapons had arrived an hour earlier in a diplomatic pouch aboard another flight, that matter arranged by the CIA chief of station in Nassau. Carter had also borrowed some of the man's clothes.

He relaxed in the back seat of the car as it headed into town and let his mind wander, a luxury he had not permitted himself since that night on the island.

No one on the big island had paid any attention to the fireworks on St. Anne's, because they themselves were having an independence day celebration, or something. Whatever was being celebrated, St. Anne's Island Resort could have blown sky high and no one would have paid any attention.

It was odd being back in Washington like this without Sigourney, Carter thought as they crossed into the city on the Arlington Memorial Bridge. Traffic was very heavy around the Watergate across from the Lincoln Memorial, but Carter let himself drift back to the island, to the ten days he and Sigourney had had together.

The driver broke into his thoughts.

"Would you care to stop by your apartment first, Mr. Carter?"

Carter looked up and shook his head. "No," he mumbled.

"Yes, sir," the driver said.

AXE headquarters occupied a building on Dupont Circle under the cover of Amalgamated Press and Wire Services. They parked in the underground garage beneath the building, and after passing through several security checks, Carter went up to David Hawk's office. He again was passed through security, Hawk was buzzed, and Carter went in.

David Hawk was a short man in his sixties. A wide head with a thick shock of white hair sat atop a moderately husky frame. In his day he had been a very tough operative. Even now he hadn't lost much of his edge. He put his ever-present cigar down and got up.

He studied Carter for several long moments in silence, then shook his head and indicated a chair. "I'm sorry, Nick."

Carter sat down. "Yeah."

"You had no warning?"

"None other than your call, sir," Carter said. It was difficult sitting there like that. He wanted to be out chasing down the U.N. lead.

"There was an overflight of two Cuban Air Force helicopters south of our installation at Guantánamo Bay around four in the morning," Hawk said. He sat down and flipped open a file folder. "One hour before that, the body of a Cuban national who worked in the Soviet embassy in Havana was dumped outside the front gate at Guantánamo. He had been shot twice at close range."

"So?"

"He was the one who provided us with the information about Ganin."

One puzzling item in the whole business came suddenly

clear to Carter, and he sat forward. "It was Ganin, and he is after me."

Hawk nodded. "It's what we figured, Nick. Ganin is too sharp to have made such a mistake. The information was planted. They were taunting us."

"They had no intention of killing me on St. Anne's. They were simply after Sigourney."

"He wants you to come after him," Hawk said. "But why? You've never had any dealings with the man."

"I don't know," Carter said. He thought back to the dead Cuban on the beach. Lashkin at the U.N. Was he the key? Was Ganin working for this Lashkin? And if that were the case, what or who was the man, that he was going to such lengths to come after one AXE operative?

"What about the attack force, Nick?"

"They were Cubans."

"You took out three of them?"

"Yes, sir."

"Did you get to question any of them?"

Carter held his silence for a long time. He had never lied to David Hawk. He had never thought such a thing possible, but at that moment he seriously considered it. Ganin was after him. So be it. But the bastard had killed an innocent woman. Either Ganin, or whoever directed the Soviet operative, was responsible. And they would pay.

"I see," Hawk said softly. He turned in his chair and looked out the window toward the Dupont Plaza Hotel across the circle. "I understand how you feel, Nick. Believe me, I do. But you must understand that we are a nation of laws."

"I understand, sir," Carter said. In his mind he was flipping the mattress over and seeing Sigourney's body for the first time.

"We have our charter, within which our operations are limited. There are certain things we can do, and there are others we cannot," Hawk said. He turned back. "If we operate under the law, then we can all sleep at night. We can know that what we are doing is morally correct. Our jobs are necessary.''

Carter kept hearing his own words over and over again in his mind: I want you to stay here, in this room, no matter what happens. Christ, he had killed her. She had trusted him. She had . . . loved him.

''If we use their methods, if we run off with a total disregard for an individual's rights, then we become one of them,'' Hawk continued.

Carter's head came up, and he met Hawk's eyes. ''I believe I still have fifteen days left on my vacation, sir,'' he said evenly.

Hawk's eyebrows rose, but he nodded. ''You do.''

''I'd like to take them.''

A fragile stillness seemed to descend over the office. Hawk's lips were pursed, his hands folded together in front of him on the desk. There was so much Carter wanted to say at that moment. But he knew that anything he would say would only serve to worsen an already bad situation. The man across the desk from him was more like a father to him than any man Carter had ever known. There was no person on this earth whom Carter had more respect for than David Hawk. But Sigourney . . . she shouldn't have suffered for this business. For all her toughness, for all her bravado, she was one of the innocents.

''Where would you go . . . if I allowed you to finish the remainder of your leave?'' Hawk asked.

Carter considered his answer in light of the manner in which Hawk had asked the question. His boss was being straightforward with him.

''New York, first.''

''And then?''

Carter shrugged. ''I honestly don't know, sir. Europe, possibly. Back to the Caribbean.''

"The Soviet Union?"

"As a private citizen . . . possibly."

"In two weeks you would be back?"

Carter nodded.

"During that time, you would not be asking for help?"

"Perhaps I might make a call from time to time, for information. But no covert help, as such."

"You would be on your own."

Again Carter nodded.

Hawk reached out to the telephone console on his desk. Carter suddenly realized that the tape recorders that normally operated whenever Hawk was speaking with someone in his office had been turned off. Hawk was reaching for the switch. His hand hovered over the button.

"Is it that important to you, Nick?" he asked.

Carter looked down at his hands. "Yes . . . she was, sir."

Hawk flipped the switch, the tape recorder's green jewel light winked on, and he looked up.

"You still have a bit more than two weeks on your leave, Nick. I suggest you get yourself off somewhere and relax. There'll be a lot of work for you when you get back."

Carter got to his feet, his eyes never leaving Hawk's face. "Yes, sir," he said. "Thank you." He turned and went to the door.

"Nick," Hawk said.

Carter turned back. "Sir?"

"I spoke with Sigourney's father. He understands. He'd like to see you . . . later."

A heaviness clamped down on Carter's chest. "Yes, sir. I had intended to talk to him when I returned from my leave."

"Good luck," Hawk said, and Carter turned and left the office.

He took the elevator down to Operations, where he stepped into his office and closed the door. At the desk that he used between assignments, he keyed his computer terminal, fed in the proper identification and codes for access to the agency's restricted data banks, and asked for available information on Arkadi Konstantinovich Ganin, and anything on the name Lashkin connected with the United Nations in New York.

While he was waiting for the information to come up, he opened his desk and took out a pack of his special cigarettes, lit himself one, then put in a call to AXE's armorer.

"N3 here. I need a couple of gas pellets."

"In connection with what assignment, sir?" the man asked.

"Clear it with Hawk," Carter snapped. "I want them here in my office in fifteen minutes." He slammed the telephone down.

The computer screen began filling with information on Ganin. According to the preface, it was mostly speculation. There was no known description, although whoever had entered the report on the computer estimated a man of Ganin's reputed abilities would probably be no younger than thirty, and certainly no older than fifty. Listed were a dozen probable assignments attributed to the Soviet operative, all of them spectacular but many of them contradictory. In one instance, Ganin supposedly assassinated a general in the Chinese army in Peking, and yet within six hours he was credited with kidnapping two people in Athens. Impossible.

The latest entry showed that Ganin was probably connected with the new Soviet assassination bureau—Komodel—and had probably participated in an operation on St. Anne's Island involving an AXE operative.

Nothing new there. Ganin was a mystery man. Not so Lashkin, for whom the computer had a lot of data.

Petr Sergeiovich Lashkin was born in Leningrad in 1935, which made him fifty-one now. He had attended Moscow State University, studied law, and then had joined the army as party adviser. Later he was recruited into the KGB and began his overseas postings. At the moment the man was number two in KGB operations out of the U.N., under the cover of adviser to the Soviet's Security Council delegation. He was married and had two children; his family lived in Moscow. In New York he was living with his secretary, Lydia Borasova, a woman in her late twenties, in an apartment in Murray Hill off East 36th Street.

Several photographs came up on the printout, showing Lashkin to be a heavyset man with thick dark eyebrows, wide-set eyes, and ponderous Slavic features. There was one photograph of Lydia Borasova, a good-looking blonde.

Carter ripped the photos from the machine and stuffed them into his pocket.

The door opened and Rupert Smith, head of Operations, stuck his head in. "We all heard, Nick. We're sorry."

Carter looked up and nodded absently. "Thanks, Smitty."

"Are you back, or are you leaving again?"

"I'm leaving in about five minutes," Carter said. He flipped off the terminal and got up.

Smitty glanced at the machine. "Lashkin's name is flagged. Your query came up on my terminal."

"Something I should know?"

"Are you on to something that *I* should know about?" AXE's Operations chief asked. He was a very sharp individual. He and Carter got along well, and the man never pulled any punches.

"Not officially."

Smitty seemed to consider the answer for a moment. "Unofficially, then, I thought you'd better know that Lashkin is being posted back to Moscow."

"Has he left yet?" Carter snapped, coming around his desk.

"Not for a couple of days, as far as we heard. He evidently has things to clear up with the Security Council. Are you going after him?"

Once again Carter found himself in the position of having to consider lying to an old friend. He didn't like it, but Ganin had neatly maneuvered him into the corner.

"Don't ask."

Smitty hesitated a moment. "Have you spoken with Hawk?"

"A few minutes ago."

A young assistant from Armory came up and Smitty stepped aside. Carter took the small package containing two of the deadly gas bombs, and the young man left.

Smitty wanted to say something else, but he just shook his head. "Good luck, Nick."

"Thanks," Carter said. He brushed past his colleague and started across toward the elevators.

"Don't go off half-cocked," Smitty called to him.

Carter glanced over his shoulder.

"Watch your back, Nick."

"Right," Carter said.

Carter took a cab to his apartment in Georgetown, where he showered, changed clothes, and packed a few things in an overnight bag. Afterward he fixed himself a sandwich and a beer, and while he sat at the kitchen table he methodically cleaned and oiled Wilhelmina, cleaned and oiled his stiletto, and taped one of the gas bombs high on his inner thigh, where it nestled like a third testical.

Normally when he traveled, his weapons went into a large cassette recorder/radio. He was bringing the radio along this time as well, but he would be wearing his weapons. He was not going to get caught short in New York.

The last time he had been in his apartment, Sigourney had cooked him a wonderful meal. Afterward they had lain in each other's arms. The memory just then was very painful for him, hardening his resolve to go after Ganin and whoever was running him.

Finished with his tasks, he called ahead to have his car pulled out of storage and readied. An hour and a half later he was heading out of Washington, D.C., on Interstate 95 toward New York City, the restored Jaguar XK-E purring smoothly, the radio playing soft music, and hard thoughts marching through his mind one after the other.

By two he had gotten around Baltimore with its heavy traffic and bad highways; by three, Trenton; and a few minutes after four, driving hard all the way, he passed under the Hudson River through the Lincoln Tunnel.

Crosstown traffic was heavy, so it was nearly five before he made it to the U.N. complex and managed to find a parking place across the street from the Secretariat Building.

Already a number of the diplomats and staff people were leaving work for the day. Carter pulled out the photographs of Lashkin and his secretary, studied them, then sat back to watch and wait.

One thought had nagged at the back of his mind on the trip from D.C. Lashkin was not a man of enough clout to run an operative such as Ganin. Which meant that either Lashkin was a red herring, or the man's cover was even better than had been thought.

The Cuban on the beach at St. Anne's, knowing his life was probably over, had spit out Lashkin's name. What did it mean?

It was barely five-thirty when Carter spotted the KGB officer and his live-in secretary coming through the gate, and he sat up.

It was definitely Lashkin; there was no mistaking him even from this distance.

He and the woman were saying something to each other, and then they climbed into the waiting cab.

Carter started his car and was about to pull out when he spotted a dark gray Chevrolet turning up First Avenue from 42nd Street. It pulled in behind Lashkin's cab, and as they passed, Carter got a good look at both men. They were husky, their features heavy. Definitely Russian. Lashkin had bodyguards.

When there was a break in traffic, Carter slammed the car in gear and hurried after Lashkin and his entourage.

They turned on 45th Street, and three blocks later headed back south on Lexington Avenue, Carter just making the light behind them. There was little doubt in his mind that Lashkin and the woman were heading to their apartment, but now it was a question of just how closely the two gorillas would stick with their charge. He decided it would give him a certain perverse pleasure to go through them, though he didn't want to make waves this early in the game. He simply wanted to talk to Lashkin, find out what his part was in the business, and if possible, confirm that it was indeed Ganin who had struck on St. Anne's. Afterward . . . Carter let the thought trail off.

At 36th Street they pulled up at the corner, Lashkin and the woman getting out of the cab, the gray Chevrolet holding back.

Carter passed them slowly, and in the next block pulled into a loading zone, jumped out of his car, and hurried back.

Lashkin and the woman had just turned the corner, and they went into a small apartment building. The gray Chevrolet came around the corner and pulled up at the curb, and one of the men got out. The car pulled away and continued down the block, while the bodyguard lit a cigarette and looked across the street. It looked as if he would be staying there for a while. Most likely the other bodyguard would park the car somewhere, then take up station at the rear of the building.

According to the computer's data, Lashkin's apartment was on the top floor of the four-story building, at the front. He and Lydia Borasova would be saying their tearful good-byes now, with Lashkin scheduled to return to his wife in a couple of days. They'd probably prefer to be alone. With luck they'd remain upstairs in their apartment for the night.

Carter crossed the street, and at the corner of the next block he pulled up short as the gray Chevy pulled into a parking spot. The driver got out, locked the door, then crossed the street and went through a gate that led through a brick wall. Evidently there was a rear access to Lashkin's building.

Carter glanced at his watch. It would be dark soon. He wouldn't be able to do much until then, except get ready and decide what he was going to do.

One goon was in the front, one in the back. Lashkin was well covered. Carter walked back to his car, got in, and found a legal parking place on the next block. He found a quiet corner in a local bar and had a drink.

Ganin and his people had come ashore and killed Sigourney. They had had a chance to kill him as well, but they did not. A mistake, or on purpose? One of the troops got left behind. Another mistake, or part of the plan? Under questioning, the man blurted out Lashkin's name.

How much of it was a setup? Carter wondered. And if this *was* some sort of an involved scheme to maneuver Carter into a vulnerable position, how much farther would it go?

Lashkin would have some of the answers. And tonight, he'd talk.

FIVE

Carter had dinner at a small restaurant on 38th Street, checked his car, and was back on Lashkin's block a little past eight. He walked past the corner where Lashkin's building was located and glanced up at the windows. Lights shone. They were presumably still up there. The one bodyguard stood out front in the shadows.

Around the corner he passed the gate, and then making sure no one was coming, he hoisted himself up over the brick wall and looked down into the courtyard.

The second bodyguard was nowhere in sight. But there were enough bushes and even a couple of trees to conceal him from Carter's vantage point.

A cab turned the corner and came down the street as Carter pulled himself the rest of the way over the wall and dropped down into the courtyard. He crouched in the shadows for a full two minutes, every sense alert for the presence of the bodyguard, for the sound of an alarm. But there was nothing.

At length, he pulled out his stiletto, and keeping low, he moved away from the wall, deeper into the courtyard, the back of the neighboring brownstone to his left, and the backs of other apartment buildings looming overhead straight across.

Carter slowly circled around to the right, but hearing a noise just ahead of him, he stopped in his tracks. It had sounded like a metallic crackle, or a hiss.

"Nothing here," someone said in Russian. The voice obviously came from a walkie-talkie.

The courtyard bodyguard murmured some reply that Carter could not make out, though he could tell the man was very close. Possibly fifteen or twenty feet away. A siren sounded somewhere down toward 34th Street.

Carter inched forward, then stopped again as a match flared just beyond a bronze statue. A moment later cigarette smoke drifted back to him. The bodyguard grunted, then moved to the left of the statue and sat down on the low bench, his back to Carter.

Gripping the stiletto lightly in his right hand, never taking his eyes off the big Russian, Carter silently stepped past the statue and directly up to the man.

At the last moment the Russian, sensing he was no longer alone, started to turn, but by then it was too late for him. Carter flipped his stiletto over and, gripping the haft firmly in his right hand, clipped the man sharply at the base of his skull behind his right ear.

The Russian's head snapped forward, his body went slack, and he slumped down onto the grass, his eyes fluttering, his left leg twitching.

Working swiftly now, Carter sheathed his stiletto, stepped around the bench, pulled off the Russian's tie and belt, and trussed the man's arms and legs together at his back. The man was just coming around as Carter stuffed a handkerchief into his mouth.

"Listen to me, comrade," Carter said in Russian. "I wish you no harm."

The Russian came fully awake, and for a moment or two he

struggled against his bonds. But it was no use. He settled down.

"That's better," Carter said, continuing to speak in Russian. "If you move, if you try to escape, I will come back and surely kill you. Do you understand?"

The Russian looked up at Carter, his eyes narrowed. But he nodded.

"Very good. It will only be a few minutes, I promise you. Be a good boy now."

The Russian was a pro. He was studying Carter's face, making sure that if and when he got out of this, he would be able to provide an accurate description.

"My name is Nick Carter. I want you to know that, comrade. I wish Comrade Ganin to know that as well. Tell him I was here."

The Russian's expression did not change.

Carter reached inside the man's coat and withdrew his wallet. He flipped it open and in the dim light studied the diplomatic identification. The man's name was Yuri Pavlovich Mosolov. He was assigned as a trade specialist with the Soviet delegation to the U.N. Carter returned the man's wallet, then straightened up and hurried across the courtyard to Lashkin's building. The rear door was secured only with a simple tumbler lock, which Carter picked in less than twenty seconds.

Inside, a dimly lit corridor ran the length of the building. In front was the elevator, but to the right of where Carter stood just within the doorway, there was a flight of stairs.

He hurried to the top floor, checked to make sure no one was in the corridor, then went down to the front apartment and listened at the door.

Music was playing softly from within, and Carter thought he heard a woman laughing.

He stepped aside, out of the range of the peephole in the door, and knocked loudly.

The music stopped a moment later.

Carter knocked again. "Comrade Lashkin," he said urgently in Russian.

"Who is it?" a man's voice asked from the other side of the door. "Who is there?"

"It is me . . . Mosolov. Open, hurry!"

"Yuri Pavlovich?" the man said, unlocking the door.

Carter pulled out his Luger, and as the door came open, he pushed his way inside.

Lashkin was shoved aside, and he cried out in alarm. Carter brought up Wilhelmina as he closed the door behind him.

"Believe me when I tell you that I do not want to shoot you, Petr Sergeiovich, but I will if you do not cooperate," Carter snapped in Russian.

The apartment was small but very tastefully decorated. Lydia Borasova, wearing only a filmy negligée, appeared in the doorway from the bedroom.

"Petr . . ." she started to say, but then her hand came up to her mouth and she stepped back.

"Get back out here, Miss Borasova," Carter ordered.

She hesitated. She was obviously very frightened.

"Who are you? What do you want with us?" Lashkin asked.

"Nick Carter. I have come here to talk with you about Arkadi Ganin."

Lashkin turned white, and he stumbled backward, off-balance, as if he were on the verge of collapse.

Carter motioned for Lydia to come out. "I don't want to hurt either of you, but I will if I have to," he said.

The woman came the rest of the way out into the living room, and she and Lashkin sat down together on the couch.

Lashkin, suddenly conscious that his girl friend was nearly naked, looked up. "Let her put on something decent."

"Your friend was not so considerate of *my* girl friend," Carter said harshly. "She stays."

Lashkin wanted to protest, but he was too frightened. "I don't know this . . . Arkadi Ganin of whom you speak."

"Yes, you do. He was most recently in Cuba under the cover name Hildebrandt. Does that name mean anything to you, comrade?"

Lashkin started to shake his head, but Lydia touched his sleeve. He looked at her.

"Tell him, Petr, and then he might go," she said. She was a very good-looking woman, with an intelligent face.

"Shut up," Lashkin hissed.

"If you value your life, comrade, you will listen to her. She is making sense."

"Either you kill me, or . . . they do it. Either way I lose," Lashkin said fatalistically.

"You die here and now, or live to take your chances another day. Your choice," Carter said.

Lashkin held his silence.

"Petr?" Lydia said in a small voice.

"What do you want of me? I know this Hildebrandt. He was here in New York a few days ago. So what?"

"Here to see you?"

Lashkin just looked at him for a moment in stony silence. "He came to my office. He spoke with me. All right?"

"About what, comrade? What did Hildebrandt wish to tell you?"

Again Lashkin was reticent.

Carter prompted him. "You are number two in the KGB hierarchy here. I know that, so let's not tell lies now."

"He checked in with me, that's all," Lashkin blurted.

"Was he running an operation here in New York?"

"Not that I was aware of," the KGB officer said. He glanced at Lydia, who had an odd, frightened look in her eyes.

"It's standard procedure for visiting operatives to check in with you?"

Lashkin looked back at Carter. He nodded. "Yes. We

don't want—'' He realized he was going too far, and he clamped it off.

Carter just looked at him.

"Hildebrandt was here. I have told you what you wanted to know, now get out of here," Lashkin said finally.

"What did he look like?" Carter asked.

Lashkin shrugged. "I don't know. Tall, dark. He was quite a good-looking fellow. I really didn't look at him that closely."

"That man was Arkadi Ganin. I believe you know that name," Carter said.

Again Lashkin paled, and his hand shook as he wiped beads of sweat from his upper lip. "I don't know this . . . Ganin. I have never seen him."

"Yes, you have. Just a few days ago, here in New York. He told you why he was here?"

"He was just passing through."

"To do what?"

"I don't know. I swear to you! I think he was merely establishing a trail. A track."

"Why would he do that, unless he wanted someone to follow him? Why, comrade?"

"I don't know."

"Where did he stay?"

"The Grand Hyatt, I think."

"How long was he here?"

"A couple of days, that's all."

"And then?" Carter asked.

"He took a plane to Cuba, and that's all I know!"

Carter stepped around the couch and went to the windows that looked down on the street. Lashkin and the woman turned and watched him. He edged the curtain aside and glanced down. There was no one there. The bodyguard was gone.

Lashkin had started to rise when Carter turned back. He stopped, Lydia's hand on his arm. There wasn't much time.

If the front guard discovered his partner had been compromised, they'd both be on their way up.

Carter flipped the Luger's safety to the off position and stepped aside so that he had a clear shot both at the door and at Lashkin.

"Who did this Hildebrandt say he worked for?"

"He didn't say," Lashkin replied. He was obviously lying.

"There isn't much time, comrade. If your people start coming through that door, someone is bound to get hurt. Them, you, perhaps your lady friend here?"

"Tell him," Lydia prompted.

"Shut up!" Lashkin said.

The front door burst open. Carter swiveled as the two Russian bodyguards barged in, their weapons raised.

Carter fired twice, catching the lead man in the chest, the two shots driving him backward into the corridor against the second man, who snapped off a shot that went wild, bringing down some plaster from the living room ceiling.

The girl screamed, and Lashkin leaped over the couch.

Carter stepped aside, fired one shot to his right, catching Lashkin high on his chest, just below his throat, then pulled around once again and fired another shot, this one blowing the second bodyguard's forehead completely off, blood spurting out of the man's eyes, bone and bits of brain and hair splattering the corridor wall as he was flung backward.

Both guards were dead; there was little doubt of it. Carter spun back to Lashkin, whose body was draped backward over the couch. He was clawing at the terrible wound below the base of his neck as he tried to breathe, blood bubbling from the wide, dark hole.

Lydia was sobbing in terror, trying to help him, but it was clear he was going to die.

"It was Kobelev!" she rasped. "He engineered this! He sent Ganin after you!"

Impossible. Kobelev was dead. Carter had seen him die

with his own eyes. She was lying. "He's dead!"

"No," she said. "He is alive. He has started Komodel with Ganin. They are waiting for you."

"Where?"

"Europe, somewhere in Europe."

A siren sounded outside in the distance. Someone had reported the shooting. Carter raced to the door. No one moved in the corridor. He turned back, hesitating a moment longer. Was the woman the key to this thing? There was no time. He could not take her with him.

"How do you know this? Who told you Ganin was working for Kobelev?"

"*He* did, you bloody fool!" Lydia shouted in English. "Hildebrandt was Ganin. He was here. He talked to me, told me that he was going to kill your girl friend, and that you would be coming."

Lashkin gasped his last breath, and his body went slack, sliding off the couch to the floor. Lydia looked down at him. "It's too late for us now," she murmured.

Carter did not want to get trapped there. He did not want a forced shoot-out with the police, nor did he want to be held.

He slammed the door, locking it, and slipped the security chain in place. Lydia was watching him wide-eyed.

"Take me with you!" she cried, stepping over Lashkin's body.

Carter brushed past her and raced into the back bedroom, where he threw open the casement window. The fire escape led down into the courtyard. No one was down there, yet, but the sirens were close now, and there were a lot of them.

"He'll kill me!" Lydia cried. "Take me with you! Please! Don't leave me here!"

Carter turned back to her. Was she the key? Was she the bait Ganin had set for him? Europe, she had said. Kobelev and Ganin. Was it possible? It made his head swim. He was there when Kobelev died! He had seen it with his own eyes!

Lydia had torn off her negligée and was pulling on a pair of slacks that had been lying on the floor. Her breasts were large and well formed, with dark pink nipples erect now that she was frightened.

He *had* been maneuvered! Kobelev had once been called "the puppet master." This was his doing. It stank of the man's perverse genius.

Carter holstered his Luger and ducked out the window onto the fire escape. Lydia leaped around the bed to the open window.

"Don't leave me!" she cried, reaching for him.

Carter eluded her grasp, looked into her eyes for a long moment, then without a word turned and scrambled down the fire escape.

At the bottom, he leaped down to the courtyard and looked up, but the blond head was gone. Europe, she had said. She was the bait. The Cuban with his dying breath had named Lashkin, leading Carter to New York. But it was the woman who had Ganin's information.

The sirens were out front as Carter hurried across the courtyard, through the gate, and down to the corner.

Police cars were coming up the street as he ducked into the shadows of a recessed doorway. When they passed, he continued around in a wide circle to where he had parked his car, then headed back out of the city, this time going north, toward the Adirondacks and a refuge.

Arkadi Ganin stepped back away from the second-floor window in the apartment building across from Lashkin's just as two police cars joined the four already there. He let the curtains slowly drop back into place.

A jumble of voices came from the speaker of a portable monitor set up on the table beside the bed. Ganin listened to the police conversations picked up from the telephone in Lashkin's apartment, and from the bodyguards' walkie-talkies.

He smiled to himself, shut off the receiver, and packed it in his suitcase.

Carter had indeed been set up. The guards had unwittingly done their parts, Lashkin, the complete fool, had done his, and the girl . . . Ganin hesitated a moment. He was pleased with her. She had reacted exactly as he thought she would. She had said and done what he thought she would, even to the point of throwing herself at Carter.

But best of all, Ganin stood in awe of Kobelev. The man had predicted every single maneuver in a delicate ballet. Even the finer nuances, such as Carter not killing Mosolov in the garden. Instead he had simply knocked the man over the head, tied him up, and had gone in. It was—Ganin, thinking now in English, groped for the word—it was quaint, definitely naïve. But it was exactly as Kobelev had predicted it would be.

Finished, Ganin pulled on his jacket, checked the tiny efficiency appartment a second time to make sure he had left nothing incriminating, and then, his single suitcase in hand, left the back way.

It was still early. There was plenty of time for his overseas call, plenty of time for a good night's sleep on his flight to Paris.

More sirens were converging on the apartment building. Soon—but not soon enough—the police would expand their search for the killer. Carter was well away, though. Ganin had to chuckle to himself. If the American had not been successful in his efforts to escape, Ganin had planned on stepping in and somehow lending a hand.

Two blocks from the apartment Ganin hailed a cab and took it over to the Tudor, a hotel just around the corner from the U.N.

After he checked in, he went back out, walking aimlessly for several blocks until he came to a telephone booth where he placed a credit card call, under the name Hildebrandt, to a number in Helsinki, Finland.

It was answered on the third ring by a gruff-voiced man speaking English. "Yes."

"It's Bruno," Ganin said softly despite the transatlantic hiss and signal loss. Signal-enhancing equipment, along with voice-print analyzers, were attached to the line.

There was a hollow silence on the line while the electronic identification procedures were automatically carried out by the equipment in the basement of a Helsinki apartment house.

Fully sixty seconds after the call was answered, another connection was made, a distant telephone began ringing, and Ganin stiffened slightly.

This time the line was answered on the first ring. "You're leaving within the hour, is that correct?"

It was Kobelev. He knew.

"Yes."

Again there was a silence on the line. Ganin could almost visualize Kobelev at his desk. He would be hopping from foot to foot, the metal plate in the back of his skull glinting dully. He would look the fool at this moment, excited as he was. He was anything but.

"He is activated," Ganin said. "It was exactly as you predicted it would be. It is only a matter of time now."

"No variations on the theme?"

"None. It was *exactly* as you said it would be. Exactly."

"I know him, you must understand. I know his soul. He was mine—he was in my grasp at one time."

Ganin was afraid the man might say something compromising over the open line. "I will go ahead. I will be there when he arrives."

"Yes, you will, Arkadi," Kobelev said.

Ganin couldn't believe that Kobelev had used his name. Chances were, the line was not being monitored, at least not from the New York end. But in Finland it would be dangerous. Or . . . was Kobelev playing even a deeper, more devious game? After all, the girl was the loose end. Kobelev had predicted Carter would not kill her, and he specifically forbade Ganin from silencing her. Were there plans within plans? Kobelev had carefully maneuvered Carter into this situation. Was he also playing with Ganin?

"You will call me from Paris and let me know the next stage," Kobelev said.

Ganin hung up.

SIX

It was past ten by the time Carter finally cleared the city and took to the secondary roads that led northwest into the Adirondack Mountains. The night was very dark, and fifty miles north of the city, traffic had thinned to only an occasional car or truck.

He lit a cigarette and settled back as some of the tension began to dissipate. He was hurt, he was confused, and he was wary of the apparent ease with which he had been maneuvered.

Sigourney's murder had only been the teaser, the one act guaranteed to get his attention, the one thing that would bring him out in the open.

In New York, Lashkin had been another ploy, there only to lead him to Lydia, who provided him with the notion that Kobelev was still alive. Kobelev, the puppet master, was the driving force behind the new Komodel. Kobelev, the master spy, was running Ganin. If it were true that Kobelev was still alive and was running Ganin, they would be a nearly unbeatable combination.

As he drove, Carter's mind went back to his nearly fatal

encounters with the Russian, the first one five years earlier
aboard the *Akai Maru*, an oil tanker bound for the West
Coast.

Kobelev's diabolical scheme had involved the radioactive
material Strontium 90, with which the tanker's load of oil had
been contaminated. Had the shipment reached the refineries
in California, and had it been refined into gasoline, hundreds
of thousands of people would have been contaminated.

As it turned out, the shipment was intercepted, but several
good people had been killed, and Carter had vowed to stop
the man.

By then Kobelev had risen high within the ranks of the
KGB, and when it was rumored that he would soon be
promoted to head the Komitet, Carter was assigned to go
after him.

Hawk's dangerous plan was to set Carter up as a traitor.
Carter would defect to the Russians, offering his services to
Kobelev himself. When he got close enough to the man, and
in a position where he could manage an escape, he would pull
the trigger.

Against an ordinary man the scheme would have worked,
but Kobelev had been ahead of them every step of the way.

Carter had defected, had been accepted by Kobelev, and
had been sent to Europe on a test mission in which he was to
kill the child of a CIA operative whom Kobelev wanted to
turn.

Once the Killmaster had proved himself, Kobelev's plan
was to have Carter return to the States to assassinate the
President.

In the end, however, Kobelev had shown his true colors.
He murdered his own wife in front of Carter's eyes, and then
Kobelev's beautiful daughter murdered her father in retribu-
tion. Or so Carter thought.

Carter could still see her at the foot of the stairs in
Kobelev's *dacha* outside Moscow, plunging the blade of a

knife into her father's back. He would see Kobelev going down, the life ebbing from his body.

Carter and Tatiana Kobelev had run, escaping from the Soviet Union. Back in the States, the girl was to point out the Soviet operative who would assassinate the President. Instead, at the last moment, she pulled out a gun and very nearly succeeded in killing the President herself. Carter had stopped her with one bullet from his Luger, downing her but not killing her.

He skirted Albany and pushed on to the northwest, stopping sometime after midnight for gasoline and something to eat at an all-night truck stop. He was tired, mentally as well as physically. In his mind's eye two visions kept alternating like flashing neon signs. The first was Sigourney's body, and the second was his final confrontation with Kobelev.

AXE used Kobelev's daughter as bait to lure the Russian out of the Soviet Union. And it had worked, to a point, though his coming out was well prepared, his field intelligence was superb, and the troops he surrounded himself with were the very best in all of the Soviet Union.

The end had come aboard the Orient Express on its final leg into Istanbul, high in the mountains of Bulgaria. It had been winter then. Carter had killed Tatiana Kobelev on that mission, and he and Kobelev were in a duel to the death atop a car of the speeding train, the Russian agent set on revenge. Suddenly the timbers of a bridge had rushed at them. At the very last moment, Carter had dropped down. Kobelev's back had been to the bridge.

"You can't fool me—" Kobelev's words had been cut off by the sickening thud of wood against bone. He was slammed facedown on the car, the back of his head little more than a raw flap of skin and bone. Carter, who was sprawled only a few feet away, had reached out to hold the body, but before he could get a grip, the vibration of the train had moved it to the edge, and it had slipped out of his grasp. Kobelev had hit the ground below and rolled into the icy froth of the river.

Then the water had its way, tumbling and smashing the body against the rocks, burying it in torrents of foam.

Was it possible that Kobelev had survived? Carter asked himself for the hundredth time, his thoughts coming back to the present. It was nearly impossible to believe, and yet the man had fooled them all before.

If it were so, if Lydia Borasova was telling the truth, if Kobelev and Ganin were working together, it would end this time. He would make sure of it. No matter what, it would end this time.

It was nearly dawn by the time Carter reached the McCauley Mountain ski area north of Albany, then turned down a narrow gravel road that led back to Little Moose Lake.

Several years earlier, Hawk had confided to Carter that he owned a small cabin retreat on the remote lake. No one within AXE, or anywhere else for that matter, knew of the existence of the place except for Carter. It was the one place in the world sacrosanct to Hawk. It was a place Carter had run to once before. Sooner or later he knew that Hawk would show up, once his boss realized that Carter had dropped out of sight.

The next step would be Europe, Carter figured. But now he needed time to think. Time to slow things down. When the confrontation came, he wanted it on his own terms. He did not want to barge in out of balance. It was what Kobelev and Ganin were trying for.

A half hour later he made the final turn down a narrow, rutted lane, emerging at length into a small clearing at the water's edge in the middle of which stood Hawk's cabin, a small, ramshackle affair.

Carter switched off the engine and the headlights, and sat

for a long time, watching the sun come up and feeling, for the first time in days, at least a small measure of peace. Here was a place of order, of authority. Hawk's indefinable stamp of personality and power was everywhere. It was comforting just now.

After a while Carter got out of his car, lit a cigarette, and walked down to the lakeshore. A fish jumped out toward the middle somewhere, the ripples of its movement expanding outward.

Had he made a mistake, Carter asked himself, in falling in love with Sigourney? Had he left himself open to attack? Had he become vulnerable?

The noise of a helicopter came to him on the gentle breeze somewhere from the south. He looked up, startled out of his introspection in time to see the machine swooping in low across the lake.

Carter pulled out his Luger and headed in a dead run toward a stand of trees to the west of the cabin, keeping low and dodging back and forth as he ran.

How could Ganin have found out about the place? It was impossible!

The helicopter came in overhead, the wash from the rotors whipping the tree branches. Carter threw himself flat behind the trees, rolled over, and brought Wilhelmina up ready to fire.

The chopper pulled around in a tight, skidding turn, then set down gently between the cabin and the dock.

Carter pushed back farther behind the trees as the passenger door popped open and a man stepped out. For a long moment Carter just stared across at him. But then he got to his feet, holstered his Luger, and stepped away from the trees.

"Nick!" Hawk shouted over the noise of the engine.

Carter hurried across to him, and they shook hands. "How'd you know I'd be here, sir?" he asked. He glanced at the pilot, whom he recognized from AXE Operations. No one in AXE knew about this cabin except for Carter, and now this pilot. Whatever brought Hawk here so fast had to be extraordinary.

Hawk ignored the question. Instead he turned away, stuck his head through the open passenger doorway, said something to the pilot, then slammed the door, and he and Carter stepped back.

Moments later the machine rose, circled left, and then keeping low, screamed back south across the lake. When it was finally out of earshot the silence was almost deafening.

"Smitty suggested we watch Comrade Lashkin," Hawk said.

"I see," Carter said. He had gone off half-cocked. No doubt Ganin had probably watched the entire operation as well. The entire thing smelled of Kobelev's manipulations.

"I figured you might be up here," Hawk said. He looked into Carter's eyes, real feeling in his expression. "Comrade Lashkin was a draw to get you to New York. They wanted you to kill him. He was useless baggage for them. And now your next draw is Paris."

"Why Paris?"

"Bob Wengerhoff, our chief of station there, was found shot to death this morning."

The timing was wrong. It could not have been Ganin, at least Carter didn't think so. He would have bet almost anything against it. "I don't think it could have been Ganin. I'm sure he was in New York, watching the entire operation."

"A Soviet diplomatic jet took off from Kennedy shortly before ten. Bound for Paris. We alerted our office there, but Wengerhoff had apparently been under surveillance for days. They knew exactly where he would be every moment."

"Ganin wants me in Paris."

Hawk nodded. "But what did you get from Lashkin? Anything?"

"Lashkin may have been nothing more than a red herring. It was his secretary they wanted me to talk to."

"Borasova," Hawk said. "She was briefly held, but they let her go early this morning."

"Has she made contact with her embassy, or anyone at the U.N.?"

Hawk's eyes narrowed. "We're watching her, of course. But she's under house arrest by her own people. Apparently she flies out tonight, back to Moscow."

She was the key. But not the one Kobelev was expecting. The puppet master had made a mistake.

Hawk was closely watching Carter, understanding something else was coming and patient enough to wait for it.

"It's Kobelev, sir. The pupper master."

"Nikolai Fedor Kobelev?" Hawk said, incredulous.

Carter nodded.

"Impossible! You saw him die yourself."

"I thought he was dead," Carter said, turning his mind again back to the train. "He should have been dead. But there was no way to confirm it."

"Is it possible?"

Was it? Carter asked himself. Was it possible, or was Kobelev's name in itself just another lure, more bait to insure Carter's compliance?

"It's Kobelev, all right. The entire operation stinks of him." He shook his head. "Lashkin was just the bait—it was Borasova who told me it was Kobelev. Kobelev is coming after me. Kobelev is alive."

"Kobelev and Ganin," Hawk said softly. "Good Lord, what a combination." He looked up, his white hair ruffling in the breeze, and pulled out a cigar. When he had it lit, he led Carter up to the cabin, where inside he put on a pot of coffee. "The chopper will be back for me in an hour. We have until then to make some sort of an intelligent decision."

Carter pulled out the cups and a bottle of brandy from the cabinet. He laid them out, then sat down.

"This time," Hawk said, "you're not going off half-cocked. If it *is* Kobelev and Ganin, you're going to have to be careful. More than that, you're going to have to beat them at their own game."

"For that I'll need help."

"You're damned right. But unofficially. As far as our operations are concerned, you're still on vacation."

Carter sat forward fast. "You think there's a leak within AXE?" The thought was chilling.

"I'm not going to take any chances, Nick. Three times we've been up against Kobelev, and three times we've failed. This time he's got Ganin, and he's expecting on winning big. But we're going to stop him. Once and for all, we're going to stop that madman."

"He'll be coming out of the Soviet Union."

Hawk held his reply for a moment. Then he nodded slowly. "He wants you dead. But he could have had you killed with Sigourney. Possibly again in New York."

"But they didn't even try."

"Which means he's luring you. First to New York. Next to Paris."

"And beyond that to some . . . killing ground of his choice."

"Eastern Europe?"

"Possibly. Only he knows at this point. But I'm sure he'll want to be there when it happens. He'll want to see it happen."

Hawk poured them both a brandy.

"I'm going to Paris," Carter said. "But first I'm going back to New York."

"Lashkin's secretary?"

Carter nodded. "I think he's made a mistake with her. I

think she's the loose end. She was there with Lashkin to provide me with the information Kobelev wanted me to have. Now that she's fulfilled her obligation, she's being recalled home. She's our key now. I'm taking her to Paris with me.''

SEVEN

It seemed like years since Carter had slept last, and he was dead tired, but he was a driven man now that he fully understood whom he was up against and what the stakes were. He had no illusions about Kobelev. The man was crazy for revenge, but he was brilliant. If he was successful with this operation, there would be no stopping him. Sooner or later one of his outrageous schemes, one of his terrible operations, would result in a confrontation between the two superpowers.

Carter left his car at Hawk's cabin and hitched a ride with his boss to the helicopter pad on the East River just a few blocks south of the United Nations.

Hawk was to arrange cover identities and passports for Carter and the Russian woman. The plan was to take her down to Washington, and from there fly to London, where they would take the ferry across to France. Kobelev's people would be watching for Carter to fly into Charles de Gaulle or Orly outside Paris. And they would redouble their efforts as soon as it was learned that Carter had the woman. Coming down to Paris by car would throw them off.

Beyond that, Carter had his own plans that he had not discussed even with Hawk. Kobelev wanted revenge, but so did Carter.

"It won't be easy, Nick," Hawk said when they'd landed. "The man is brilliant. He'll have more tricks up his sleeve."

"I know, sir," Carter said.

They shook hands. "Good luck, then."

"Thanks."

Carter took a cab over to Penn Station, left his suitcase in a coin-operated locker, then bought two one-way tickets to Washington, D.C., on the evening train that left at eight. Their identities, passports, and travel arrangements would be ready for them when they arrived.

In a stall in the men's room he checked his weapons, then took another cab, this time to within a couple of blocks of Lydia Borasova's apartment, where he made a quick pass on foot.

There were no police cars out front, which he found mildly surprising. But Lashkin and Borasova were both Soviet diplomats, and therefore enjoyed diplomatic immunity. The Soviet delegation must have raised enough hell to make the New York police back down. And as far as Kobelev was concerned, the risk with the woman was all but over. She would be guarded by her own people.

It was just after four when he approached the apartment, this time from the north down Fifth Avenue. It was Wednesday, and the streets were crowded.

Within half a block of the apartment, he spotted the first of the Russian legmen coming around the corner from Madison Avenue.

Carter merged smoothly with a knot of people on the sidewalk, and he kept moving. The Russian stopped a moment, then, apparently realizing something, turned on his heel and walked back the way he had come. Before he disappeared around the corner, though, he scanned the street in both directions. He was definitely a pro. Carter hesitated, and feigned interest in a window display.

A couple of minutes later, still at that corner, Carter spotted the big, barrel-chested man turning the far corner.

It was a pattern. Evidently the man went back and forth in front of the apartment building, turning the corner at both ends of the block, making sure of the approaches.

Next he'd come back that way, then turn and repeat the process.

Carter quickly crossed the street and went up the steps to the Morgan Library, where he lit a cigarette and waited fully five minutes until the Russian appeared once again at the corner, looked both ways up the street, and turned back.

Immediately after the man disappeared, Carter hurried down the steps and up to the corner. The Russian was a third of the way down the block, heading slowly away, not looking back. There were several other pedestrians in the block, some traffic, and a lot of parked cars.

As far as Carter could tell, there were no other watchers. Someone would be out back. And no doubt someone was in or near the apartment with Lydia Borasova. But the approach from the street side was guarded by only the one man.

The guard stopped, then disappeared around the corner.

In the next few seconds Carter hurried to the neighboring brownstone, where at the door he buzzed all five apartments.

"Delivery for Alberts," he mumbled into the speaker grille.

A second later the door lock buzzed, and he was inside, rushing to the back stairwell where he silently raced up to the top floor.

He found the rooftop access door with no trouble, and ninety seconds after entering the building, he was on the roof keeping low and well away from the edges so that he would not be spotted from below.

The buildings on this block were all connected, and there was only a two- or three-foot difference in the heights of the rooftops. Carter jumped down to the roof of Lydia's apartment building and went to the access door, which was locked. He easily slipped the latch using Hugo's blade and silently made his way down the stairs to the top floor, hesitating just within the doorway.

No sounds came from the corridor. Carter eased the door open a crack and looked out.

A very large man with a short haircut and wearing a dark, baggy suit leaned against the corridor wall near the elevator. He was turned sideways, but was looking away.

Carter pulled out Wilhelmina, made sure the safety was off, then burst out of the door, dropping into the classic shooter's stance, the Luger up in both hands.

The Russian spun around, reaching for his weapon.

"*Nyet!*" Carter snapped urgently but keeping his voice low.

The Russian hesitated.

Carter shook his head. "Do not do it, comrade, or you will die here in this corridor," Carter said in Russian.

For several long, tense moments they stood in a tableau, frozen at opposite ends of the short corridor, the Russian obviously weighing his chances. But then the big man visibly relaxed, letting his hands fall loosely to his sides. He nodded.

Carefully Carter straightened up and moved down the corridor, motioning with his Luger for the Russian to move back up the corridor to Lydia's door.

"Is there anyone inside besides the woman?" Carter asked.

The Russian said nothing, though he moved up the corridor. He was still gauging his chances.

"I must know, comrade. If it is a lie, you will surely die."

"There is no one other than the woman," the man said.

"You have the key." Carter said it as a statement of fact.

"Open the door. I will be directly behind you."

Again the Russian hesitated, and again he made the correct decision. Carefully he reached into his coat pocket and slowly withdrew the apartment key. He turned and unlocked the door.

"Inside," Carter said, coming up behind the man.

The Russian pushed open the door, and as he moved inside he leaped forward, twisting to the right as he reached for his gun.

But Carter was right there. He lashed out with the butt of Wilhelmina, catching the big man at the base of his skull just behind his right ear.

The Russian went down like a felled steer, crashing into a small table. Lydia Borasova, wearing a bathrobe, came out of the bathroom as Carter was shoving the downed man aside and closing the door.

"Oh, my God!" she cried.

Carter looked up, and grinned. "Not exactly a sentiment Comrade Kobelev would enjoy hearing."

The woman stepped back, her hand to her mouth.

Carter stooped down to make sure the Russian was out and would stay that way for a while. Quickly he took the man's big pistol, emptied it, and shoved it under the couch. Next he pulled off the man's belt and tie and trussed him up, Lydia watching him with wide eyes.

When he was finished he straightened up. "I haven't got a lot of time to explain myself, Miss Borasova, so I'll only tell you this once," he said.

She was shivering. Carter expected that she was more frightened of what Kobelev would do to her when this was over than she was of the current situation.

"You are not returning to Moscow, at least not tonight. You're coming with me."

"Where are you taking me?"

"Paris."

"Oh . . . no," she cried. "No . . . please, I beg you! He will kill me!"

"Perhaps *I* will if you do not cooperate. And I'm here right now. Comrade Kobelev is far away."

"I cannot."

"You will," Carter snapped. "And when it's over, I promise that you will be given a choice. You'll be allowed to return to Moscow, or you will be given asylum here in the States."

She was shaking her head, but she seemed less certain than before.

"If you choose to return to Moscow, we'll make sure you'll go back blameless. You were kidnapped at gunpoint. It is your choice."

She was searching for the right decision. He could see it in her eyes. "What am I supposed to do in Paris?"

"Provide me with information I may need. Nothing more. You won't be in the line of fire if I can help it. I promise you."

She looked down at the unconscious Russian on the floor. "There are two others outside. One in front and another in the back."

"I know. We'll get away, if you cooperate."

She looked up. Her eyes softened. "Is it true that your . . . lover was killed?"

"She was burned to death," Carter said grimly. "It was Ganin."

She shook her head. "It was Kobelev. The man is insane!"

"We must leave now."

"I have your promise?"

Carter nodded.

"And if I decide that I want to return to the United States? It will be arranged?"

Again Carter nodded.

She finally came to a decision. "Yes," she said. "I will do it, if only to stop the monster."

"Get dressed and pack a single bag."

"I'm packed," she said. She turned to go to the bedroom but then stopped. "What about a passport? I cannot travel on my diplomatic documents. I would be spotted."

"Leave it here."

She looked at Carter, then nodded and went into the bedroom. He followed her.

For a moment she hesitated about undressing in front of him but then she shrugged, understanding that he could not trust her—yet. She took off her robe. She was nude beneath, her large breasts soft and womanly, her stomach smooth and flat, and her legs somewhat short but very nice.

Quickly she pulled on panties, a bra, pantyhose, and then stepped into a skirt and pulled on a blouse. At the mirror she put on some lipstick, brushed her hair, then threw her makeup things into her purse, grabbed her coat, and picked up her suitcase where it stood next to the bed.

"I am ready," she said. Her nostrils were flared and her eyes were wide. She was frightened.

"Do you have a weapon, Lydia?"

She shook her head. "No," she said. "It was not my mission."

"Which was?"

"To keep an eye on our delegation. There were certain of them . . . who were weak."

"What is your connection with Comrade Kobelev?"

For a long moment Carter didn't feel she would answer him. Her eyes became moist, and she hung her head.

"For two years . . . I was his mistress."

"Did you love him?"

"No," she snapped defiantly. "It was for my parents! He threatened to kill them if I did not cooperate!"

She was the key to Kobelev. Carter felt bad about using her

that way, but he had been honest when he promised her sanctuary after it was over. Once Kobelev found out Carter had her, it would shake him up. Maybe he would begin making his own mistakes.

At the door, Carter checked to make sure the corridor was still empty, and then they hurried to the stairs and went down to the ground floor. The guard out front was halfway up the block when Carter checked outside. He waited until the man was around the corner, and then he and Lydia hurried outside, down the stairs, and rushed to the opposite corner, where they got a cab half a block away.

"Do you think he saw us?" Lydia asked when they were safely inside.

"No," Carter said. He glanced out the rear window. No one was coming. As far as he could tell, no one was following them.

"Where to, buddy?" the cabby asked over his shoulder.

"Penn Station," Carter said.

"By train?" Lydia asked.

Carter looked at her. Was it a slip? Had they expected him to return for her? Or was he being overcautious and paranoid?

"By train," he said. "What did you expect?"

She was puzzled for a moment, but then she figured it out, and she shook her head. "If you do not trust me, I do not blame you. But I never expected to see you again. I assumed, if we are going to Paris, it would be by air, and not by rail."

Carter had to laugh. "You're right on both counts: I don't trust you, and yes, we're going to Paris, but not by train."

With a couple of hours to kill before their train left, Carter checked Lydia's bag into a storage locker next to his in the station, and then they walked across the street and down the block to an Italian restaurant on Eighth Avenue for something to eat.

She told him about her youth in Leningrad and how she had

come to be accepted as a medical student at Moscow State University. In her second year she had gone to a party with friends, who were officers in the student Communist Party organization, where she met Kobelev. The man pursued her, sending her gifts, which she returned, but later sending her parents gifts and granting special favors such as permitting them to shop in the foreign exchange stores.

"After his wife died he made me move out to his *dacha* with him," she said. "I hated it, but by then my parents could not exist without his help. There was no going back for them."

"Did he tell you how his wife died?"

She shrugged. "Cancer, I think."

"He shot her to death. I was there. I witnessed it."

"But why? He said he loved her. He missed her."

"She was in his way. There was an important assignment. He used his daughter the same way."

"I didn't know he had a daughter."

"She's dead."

"He killed her?"

"I did," Carter said.

Lydia sucked in her breath. "It is . . . a vendetta, then, between you two. You killed his daughter, he killed your lover, and now . . ." She hesitated a moment. "You two are alike?"

"No. I killed Tatiana in self-defense. She had become as desperate and as crazy as her father. I dislike killing women."

Lydia managed a wry smile. "You do not trust me, and yet you tell me of this weakness. What is to prevent me from simply getting up and walking out of here?"

"The thought that when this is over, you can be free."

She took a deep breath and let it out slowly. "I would like more coffee, please."

They made a couple of quick passes around Penn Station

before Carter was satisfied that they had not been followed. A few minutes before eight, they went inside, got their bags, and climbed aboard the train just as it was about to pull out.

After the train had emerged from the station, and the conductor had collected their tickets, they went forward to the crowded, noisy club car, where they managed to find a couple of seats near the forward door.

Carter ordered scotch for himself and vodka, neat, for Lydia. When they were settled, he lit himself a cigarette. He was very tired, but he figured he would get some sleep on the transatlantic flight.

The vision of Sigourney's body in the burned remains of the house came back to him. He knew that he would have that same picture in his mind for a very long time to come. It would haunt his dreams long after this business with Kobelev was finally resolved.

"She must have been wonderful, your lover," Lydia said softly.

Carter looked up. "It shows?"

She nodded. "It is Kobelev's specialty . . . finding one's weaknesses and brutally exploiting them. He is very good at it."

"What was your weakness?" Carter asked.

"My parents . . ." Lydia started, but then she hesitated. "That was just my excuse. I was my own weakness. I was tired of the university. I was sick to death of the other students. I wanted to be . . . loved. To be needed."

"By someone important?" Carter prompted.

"By someone important. By someone exciting. By a man."

"Kobelev was that man."

"At first. But he's a monster. There were times . . ." Again she hesitated. "There was a doctor on his staff at the *dacha*."

Carter remembered the man. He had been kind.

"Kobelev decided he no longer liked or trusted the doctor,

so he challenged him to a duel . . . with swords. The doctor pleaded with him—'I know nothing about fighting, I am a medical man,' I remember him saying. But it was no use. It took the doctor a very long time to die. I had to watch it all.''

"So you jumped at the chance to come to the States. To be his eyes and ears in New York."

"Anything to get away from him. Anything!"

Carter finished his drink and ordered another. When he sat back down, Lydia was watching him.

"What do you expect to do in Paris? You say you want information from me?"

"I was lured to Lashkin and you in New York. Now I am being lured to Paris. Kobelev wants me in Europe. He means to keep leading me along until I get to a place of his choosing where he intends to kill me."

"Paris?"

"I don't think so. But one of his people killed one of ours there."

"And you are going to Paris to kill a Russian."

"Not just any Russian. One who works for Kobelev."

"Which one?"

"It doesn't matter, as long as he is Kobelev's man."

"I am Kobelev's woman, so I will be your information bank."

Carter nodded.

"If I refuse?"

"I don't think you will."

She sighed. "No, I will not. Kobelev's people are not noted for being kind, gentle men. If they survive with him, they must be bastards too. Yes, I know of a man in Paris for you. But he is very good, and it will be very dangerous for you. Very dangerous."

"Who is he?"

"Let us get to Paris first. By then I will feel better about trusting you."

Carter had to laugh. "Fair enough."

"What then?" Lydia asked.

"By then Comrade Kobelev will know that I have you, and he will know that I have killed his man there. The next move will be his. His and Ganin's. They will send me a signal, and it will be a very clear one."

Lydia shuddered. "Ganin. He is a dangerous one."

"Do you know him?"

"I only know of him. I know he is the one man on this earth whom Kobelev respects, and in some ways fears."

EIGHT

It was almost midnight by the time Carter and Lydia reached Washington, D.C., and took a cab over to the Mariott Twin Bridges Motel across the Potomac. They checked in as man and wife, under the name Bardon, and got a first-floor room with a patio door so that they would have a second exit in case of trouble.

Word most certainly would have already gotten back to Kobelev that Carter had successfully snatched Lydia, and the reaction would be swift. Right now orders had undoubtedly gone out: Get Carter and Borasova! At all costs!

Before they had gone back to their room, Carter made a brief call to Hawk's private number, informing him where they were staying. He used the house phone as an extra precaution.

They ordered a couple of drinks and a plate of sandwiches from room service, and a half hour later Rupert Smith, AXE Operations chief, showed up. Carter let him in.

"What have you got for us?"

Smitty was looking across the room at Lydia, who had just

taken a shower and was sitting propped up in bed, wrapped only in her bathrobe. She smiled.

"Lydia Borasova, Smitty," Carter said.

"I've heard of you, Miss Borasova," Smitty said. He was obviously taken with her.

"You have me at a disadvantage, Mr. . . .?"

"Smitty is good enough," Carter said. He turned back to the Operations man. "None of this is in the daily log."

Smitty shook his head. "He told me the score." He carried a slim attaché case that he placed on the table and opened. From within he pulled out several items, the first of which were their airline tickets.

"British Airways, the Concorde," he said. "You'll be in London at four-thirty in the afternoon, local time. An XJ6 Jaguar sedan, license GK777-77, will be waiting for you in long-term parking at Heathrow . . . 5B54. In the glove compartment are your tickets for the Channel crossing. You'll leave immediately."

Carter glanced at the tickets. "In Paris?"

"You'll be at the Lancaster on the Rue de Berri near the Champs-Elysées."

"I know the hotel," Carter said.

Next Smitty pulled out their passports, international driver's licenses, and other identification papers. "You'll be traveling as husband and wife . . . Robert and Elizabeth Scott. You're an engineer from Chicago in Paris to speak with the Aerospatile people."

The passports and other papers were perfect, of course. "No one has been alerted to our coming?" Carter asked.

"Not a soul. It's just Hawk, myself, you . . . and Miss Borasova," Smitty said. He passed Carter a small vial, keeping it hidden in his hand. "This might help you sleep tonight."

Carter understood, and he nodded. "Thanks," he murmured. Then in a louder voice, ''Has there been any reaction to her disappearance?''

''Not a thing, as far as we can tell. But they know she's gone. We watched the apartment. They all left.''

''Good,'' Carter said.

Smitty studied his face for a moment. ''Would you like me to stick around outside tonight?''

Carter shook his head. ''Thanks anyway, Smitty.''

''One more thing. Hawk wonders . . . if you've given thought to Paris. Specific thought.''

''Yes, I have.''

Smitty nodded.

''Good night, Smitty. Thanks for your help.''

The Operations chief lingered a moment longer, but he knew better than to interfere in such a delicate operation when it was running. Before and after an assignment he was a stickler for detail, and for justifications. But he allowed AXE operatives a relatively free hand when they were in the middle of the fray. Wisely so.

They shook hands. ''Good luck,'' Smitty said, and he left.

Carter poured Lydia another glass of Perrier, dropping one of the powerful sleeping tablets into the glass. When it was dissolved, he brought it over to her.

''No, thank you, Nick,'' she said, looking up. She had been watching television. Some late movie on cable.

''Drink it,'' Carter insisted.

Her eyes narrowed. ''I won't run, you know. I won't telephone him. I won't betray you. I want my freedom.''

''I know,'' Carter said gently. ''But it's a little too soon for me, and there is too much at stake right now.''

She nodded. ''I understand,'' she said. She took the glass from Carter and drained it in one swallow. She handed the glass back, then rolled over and closed her eyes. ''What time does our plane leave in the morning, Mr. Scott?''

''Eight,'' Carter said. ''I'll wake you in plenty of time.''

Across the room, he poured himself a drink, lit a cigarette, then took out Wilhelmina and sat down, prepared for the long vigil.

London's Heathrow Airport was a madhouse; nevertheless, Carter and Lydia managed to clear customs and find the sleek Jaguar sedan by five-thirty. Carter had gotten a few hours sleep on the supersonic flight and he felt pretty good, although the wound in his leg was still giving him some trouble.

They made it down to Dover, driving very fast, in time for the last Hovercraft passage across the Channel to Calais. From there they took the E5 to Boulogne, then south through Abbeville and Beauvais on the long haul to Paris.

Lydia had been talkative during the trip, but as they neared Paris she quieted down, a wan note in her expression. Carter suspected she was frightened of being so close to Kobelev's operation. Frightened of her part in the plan.

"His name is Lev Ivanovich Borodin," she said when they were a few miles outside of Paris. They had been driving in silence for a long while.

Carter glanced over at her. "Kobelev's man?"

She nodded. "He works out of the Tass office as a journalist. Gives him the reason to travel around the country."

The night was overcast and very dark. There was not much traffic at that hour.

"How do you know this?" Carter asked.

"He was there . . . outside Moscow, at the *dacha*. I met him before he was posted to France. Kobelev thought highly of him. Called him his up-and-coming Red star. He has cold eyes. He is just as bad as Kobelev."

"In what way?"

"He is ruthless," she flared, looking over. "In order to be Kobelev's handmaiden you must first kill."

"Not so unusual—" Carter began, but Lydia savagely cut him off.

"A child! You must kill a child to prove you are above compassion. Even the state comes second to your loyalty to Nikolai Fedor."

Carter's trial assignment with Kobelev had been to kill the child of a CIA operative in France. "Borodin killed a child?"

"I saw it with my own eyes. She was a young girl, perhaps eight or nine, from one of the collectives outside Moscow. Kobelev just sent for her, and somehow she appeared. Borodin strangled her, slowly. He crushed her neck. He enjoyed it!"

Carter's hands were cramping up, and he realized that he was gripping the steering wheel so tightly he was losing feeling in his fingers. He loosened his grip.

Lydia's eyes were glistening. "You don't know how it was . . . how it still is."

"Will he still be in Paris? Might he have been reassigned?"

"He is still there. Kobelev doesn't move his people around until they're kicked out."

If Carter had had any qualms about simply killing a Soviet operative, they were dispelled by Lydia's story. Knowing Kobelev as he did, he did not doubt the truth of her tale.

"But listen to me, Nick. This Borodin is very good. He is intelligent, he is quick, and he is very strong."

"I'm not an eight-year-old girl he can so easily strangle."

"No, but you are tired, you have some injury to your right leg, and you have revenge in your soul because of the death of your lover. All distractions."

"What are Borodin's weaknesses?" Carter asked after a few moments of silence.

"He has none. Not even conceit."

It was four in the morning when they woke the sleepy concierge at the Hotel Lancaster, got their key, and went up to their room.

Carter unpacked his weapons in the tiny bathroom, out of

Lydia's sight, and when he emerged she was lying on the bed fully clothed except for her shoes. She was nearly asleep.

"Mmmm?" she said, half rising.

"Go back to sleep," Carter said gently. "I'm going to check outside to make sure we weren't spotted coming in."

"Don't go," she said.

"I'll be right back. In the morning you can tell me more about Borodin."

He slipped out the door before she could protest further, but he did not immediately go downstairs. Instead he waited by the door, listening. He could hear Lydia stirring, then she went into the bathroom. Moments later the toilet flushed, and he heard the bed springs creak, then nothing.

Five minutes later he turned and quietly went down the back stairs and out into the predawn darkness.

He figured he had only a couple of hours to find Borodin, do what was necessary, and then get clear. Once the dawn came, it would be impossible for him to make any overt moves against Kobelev.

Ganin was somewhere in the city. Although Carter did not know the man, had never met him, he had an empathy for him. He could feel Ganin's presence. Somewhere, watching, waiting. Somewhere in the city to lure Carter another step closer to Kobelev's killing ground.

Half a block from the hotel Carter found what he was looking for: a telephone kiosk. He managed to get a sleepy operator to respond, and he placed a credit card call to Smitty's special information number in Washington.

It took almost five minutes for the connection to be made and the proper identifications to be verified.

"Yes?" Smitty said.

"Lev Ivanovich Borodin. Works for Tass in Paris. I need his residence address."

There was a silence on the line, as if Smitty had not heard. Carter knew better.

A police car passed slowly along the avenue, the two

officers eying Carter, but they did not stop. A few minutes later Smitty was back with an address Carter recognized off Rue du Faubourg St.-Honoré, very near the British embassy, and only a dozen blocks from where he stood.

He hung up before Smitty could ask the inevitable question, pulled up his coat collar against the chill morning air, and headed down to the Rond Point and from there up past the ornate Palais de l'Elysée to St.-Honoré.

Already the early-morning delivery vans were beginning to make their rounds, and the air smelled of fresh bread and croissants.

The apartment building was a tall glass and steel affair, the sort that most Parisians hated in the center of their city, complete with a security guard in the lobby beyond locked glass doors.

Carter went around back to the service entrance, where soon—within the next hour or less—the tradesmen would begin showing up, and he rang the bell. He took out his Luger.

"*Oui*," a voice came from the speaker.

"It is me, you fool, let me in," Carter growled in very bad French, putting as much of a Russian accent into it as he could.

"Who is this? I will call the police. Go away!"

"You idiot, it is I, Borodin, of 1107! Let me in or I will have your job!"

"The front door—" the Frenchman sputtered.

"If I wanted to use the front door, I would have come in that way! Now be quick!"

If anyone showed up in the next few minutes, or if the Frenchman inside had his wits about him and telephoned security at the front door, the game would be up.

The latch clicked and the door started to open. Carter shoved his way inside, bringing Wilhelmina up into the face of a startled old Frenchman.

"*Mon Dieu!*" the man squeaked.

Inside, Carter let the door shut and lock, and backed the Frenchman up against the wall of the small office. To the right, swinging doors led to a loading dock, and straight back was a service elevator.

"Make a sound, monsieur, and you will die here tonight," Carter hissed in perfect French. The old janitor's eyes were wide, his Adam's apple bobbing. He nodded.

"You have the master key for the apartments?"

The man was too frightened to lie. He nodded again.

"And the key for the elevator?" Carter snapped. "Be quick!"

The Frenchman glanced toward the elevator, and nodded a third time.

"*Bon*," Carter said. He pulled the man around and aimed him toward the elevator. "Your keys—quickly! We are going to the eleventh floor. I wish to speak with Comrade Borodin."

The Frenchman fumbled out his keys and handed them to Carter. He and Carter stepped aboard the elevator, and Carter motioned for the man to take them upstairs.

"Which key operates this car?" Carter asked.

The white-haired Frenchman looked from Carter's eyes to the outheld keys, and pointed to one.

Carter inserted it into the elevator lock-out control, flipped it over, and the car stopped. He turned it back on, and they continued up.

Next, Carter holstered his Luger, pulled out his stiletto, and cut the emergency telephone cord.

"Now, listen to me, my old friend," he said. "I wish you no harm. I swear to God, I do not. So if you cooperate with me, and do nothing to sound an alarm, this will all be over in a few minutes, and it will be an adventure you can tell to the police, and then to your wife. You will be a hero."

The Frenchman blinked. "I do not wish to die, *monsieur*."

"And you will not, if you do as I say."

"Oui."

"I will lock you in the elevator. It will only be for a few minutes. When I am finished with my task, I will return, we shall ride together to the ground floor, and I shall leave. No noise. No alarm. Do you understand?"

"Oui, monsieur. I understand. And it will be as you say."

"Very good," Carter said.

They arrived at the eleventh floor. Carter stepped aside as the doors came open, but the corridor was empty. He flipped the key, withdrew it, and quickly stepped off the car. On the outside he inserted the key into the emergency override lock and flipped it left to Stop. Slowly the doors closed on the frightened Frenchman.

With the building's master key in one hand and Hugo gripped loosely in his left, Carter hurried down the broad, thickly carpeted corridor to Borodin's apartment.

He was taking a very large chance coming here like this. Lydia had provided him with the name. And she was Kobelev's woman. This could very well be more of the elaborate plan. It could be a setup. It was possible Borodin was not alone. Very possible.

At the door Carter listened, but no sounds came from within.

Carefully he inserted the master key into the lock and slowly turned it. The latch opened, and the door came ajar.

For several long, tense moments Carter stood stock-still, his every sense alert for another presence on the other side of the door. But there were no sounds, no movement, nothing.

Stepping aside, Carter shifted Hugo to his right hand and slowly pushed the door the rest of the way open. A narrow vestibule led into what appeared to be a wide living room. Directly across were several large windows, the curtains open, through which the lights of Paris shown dimly.

Carter stepped inside and softly closed the door behind him.

He waited in the vestibule until his eyes adjusted completely to the relative darkness. At length he could see the outlines of the couch, several chairs, what appeared to be bookcases along one wall, and an opening that probably led back to the bedroom.

The hairs at the back of Carter's neck suddenly rose. Someone was there. Very close. He started to step to one side, when something very hard slammed at him from the right, smashing into his knife arm, his fingers going numb, Hugo slipping to the floor.

He tried to move out of the way, but was hampered by a low table, which crashed over. An instant later something that felt like a battering ram smashed into the side of his head, knocking him off his feet, the night exploding into a million bursts of light.

Carter kicked the table away and rolled over as a booted foot caught him squarely in his wounded right thigh, causing him to cry out involuntarily.

He rolled again, this time the booted foot missing his head by inches, Borodin grunting with the effort.

Although Carter was stunned, it was all the opening he needed. He scrambled backward and leaped to his feet in time to counter a huge, meaty fist. In rapid order he hammered three blows to Borodin's chest, and a fourth to the side of the big man's face, sending him staggering backward against the back of the couch.

The Russian recovered instantly, charging Carter like a berserk bull elephant, the weight of his rush sending them both back crashing into the wall.

Carter brought his knee sharply up into Borodin's groin, putting every ounce of his strength into it, the air whooshing out of the Russian's lungs.

Borodin smashed his forehead into Carter's face once,

then again before Carter could twist out of his grip and stumble out of the way.

The Russian was incredible. He swiveled lightly on his feet and charged, but Carter leaped aside, his bad leg nearly collapsing beneath him. But then he was in the middle of the large living room, with much more space in which to maneuver.

The Russian paused and shook his head. He smiled. "Nikolai Fedor said you would come to me."

Had Lydia betrayed him after all? Had it been a setup?

"Two weeks ago he said you would be coming. I have been waiting!" Borodin grunted.

Two weeks ago. . . . It suddenly connected in Carter's mind. "It was you who killed Wengerhoff."

Borodin laughed. "Just as I will kill you, Carter. This time it will be my show, not Ganin's!"

The Russian leaped across the couch. It was a fatal error. For a moment the big man was off-balance, all of his weight on one leg. Carter jumped forward, slamming his foot just below the man's kneecap, Borodin's leg breaking with a loud snap.

As the Russian fell forward, bellowing in rage and pain, he managed to grab the front of Carter's coat and drag him down.

Carter twisted to the left, at the same moment shoving Borodin to the right, and suddenly he was behind the Russian, his knee in the small of the man's back, his hands on the man's forehead and chin.

"This is for the little girl you killed, you son of a bitch!" Carter swore, and he jabbed his knee harshly downward at the same moment as he yanked Borodin's head back with all of his might.

The Russian's neck snapped with an audible pop, and the man went slack, dead instantly.

Carter fell back, exhausted, battered, hurt, as he caught his breath. The Russian had been waiting for him. Kobelev had foreseen Carter's move. He had orchestrated the situation in New York and again here in Paris. It meant Ganin would be setting up the next lure. The killing ground was coming closer.

After a long time, Carter got painfully to his feet, found his stiletto, and let himself out of the apartment.

He started down the broad corridor, but it wasn't until he had gotten within ten feet of the elevator before he realized that something was wrong . . . drastically wrong.

The door of the car was open! The elevator was empty! The Frenchman had escaped!

NINE

Arkadi Ganin stood in the broad corridor just around the corner from the elevator, listening for Carter to turn and go the other way. Surely the American would not take the service elevator back down. He would have to suspect it was a trap.

Behind Ganin, lying on the floor, was the body of the old Frenchman, who had begged for his life. Ganin felt a twinge of genuine sadness for the old man who unfortunately had been in the wrong place at the wrong time. His death had been unavoidable.

Kobelev had predicted this. He had foreseen that Carter would somehow come up with Borodin's name. He predicted that the American would come here and kill the man.

The only thing Kobelev had not prophesied was Carter returning to New York to snatch Lydia Borasova. Ganin had to admire the American's cunning and skill, yet in the end it would not be enough. In the end—although he probably would not beg for his life—Carter would die.

Carter was close now. Just around the corner, barely a few feet away. Ganin raised his silenced pistol. He did not want the final confrontation to come then and there, yet he was very wary of the American, very respectful of him.

Kobelev had been nearly insane with rage earlier on the telephone. He wanted his woman back. He wanted her in Moscow so that he could strangle her to death with his own hands. He would cut her into little pieces and mail them to her parents. Then he would kill them. Anyone who had ever known or loved Lydia Borasova would die.

But not Carter.

"Listen to me, Arkadi, listen very closely. I do not want him killed yet. He must come to me first. It has all been arranged. He must come to me. He must!"

Carter turned, going the other way down the corridor. Ganin could hear him moving away, and he breathed a sigh of relief.

Seconds later the stairwell door bumped closed, and Ganin eased around the corner. The corridor was empty.

He took his set of elevator keys out of his pocket, activated the service elevator, and took it downstairs. Going out the side door, he raced around to the front of the apartment building, stopping just before the corner.

Five minutes later Carter emerged from the opposite side of the building, paused a moment, then crossed the street and hurried back toward the Champs-Elysées.

Ganin, wearing a maintenance man's coveralls, climbed into his van and headed slowly up the street behind Carter, a cigarette dangling languorously out of the corner of his mouth.

Carter rounded the corner at the Palais de l'Elysée, and Ganin sped up to catch up with him. He did not want to lose the American. Kobelev wanted another challenge thrown at him. For that they would need to know at what hotel he was staying, and whether or not he had the woman with him.

Ganin came around the corner down the Avenue Montaigne, but Carter was gone. Only a few cars were parked on the street, and there were absolutely no pedestrians.

"Damn," Ganin swore aloud. Had he underestimated the American? Without slowing his pace, and without it being obvious that he was searching for someone, Ganin continued down to the corner, then sped back toward the Place de la Concorde.

He parked the van along the side, pulled off his coveralls, threw away the cigarette, donned a wide-brimmed borsalino, and hurried on foot back the way he had come.

Carter had apparently suspected he was being followed. He had ducked in somewhere to see who came up behind him. A van. Not an Italian on foot. . . .

There was something about the maintenance man in the service van that had passed moments ago that bothered Carter. But the van had disappeared and had not come back around the block. Was he jumping at shadows?

He could feel Ganin's presence now much more strongly than before. It gave him an itchy feeling between his shoulders. Borodin had been expecting him. Did that mean Ganin was close at hand?

Carter glanced back toward St. Honoré. Had Ganin in fact been in the apartment building? Had Ganin taken the old Frenchman out of the elevator?

He took a step back, but then stopped. He was being stupid. Had Ganin been there, he'd be long gone by now. The confrontation would come, but not just then.

Carter looked down toward the Rond Point, then turned on his heel and hurried around the corner to the Avenue Roosevelt, the back way to the hotel, stopping every now and then at random intervals to duck into doorways, to bend over to tie his shoes, and see what was behind him. But if Ganin was there, he was not able to detect him.

Hawk's words kept coming back to him: *Against Ganin . . . you're going to have to be whole. No*, more *than that—you'll need a hundred and* ten *percent.*

Carter knew that he was nowhere near that. He was tired, he was battered from his encounter with Borodin, and the wound in his right leg was throbbing so badly he could hardly concentrate on anything else.

The dawn was just breaking when Carter circled his hotel twice before he slipped in the back way and hurried upstairs to his room.

He listened at the door for a moment but could hear nothing, so he let himself in.

Lydia was sitting up in bed. She was awake, a terrified look in her eyes. When she recognized who it was she sagged in relief.

"I didn't know what happened to you," she said. She made no move to get up.

Carter closed and locked the door, then went to the window and looked down at the street. Traffic was beginning to pick up with the morning, but there was no sign of the van or the maintenance man he had seen driving it.

"What is it?" Lydia asked. "What happened?"

Carter turned, and she realized that he was in pain. She shoved the covers back and jumped out of bed.

"What happened to you?" she cried.

"I'm all right," Carter said.

She helped him to the bed, took off his shoes, and helped him take off his jacket. "You went to Borodin," she said. "You killed him? You went up against him?"

Carter looked up. "He won't kill little girls again."

Lydia studied his face for a moment, then glanced at the window. "But you suspect you may have been followed. By whom?" She looked back. "Ganin?"

Carter shrugged. "He's probably here in the city." The last few days were finally starting to catch up with him. The room was beginning to go gray and soft.

He pulled out Wilhelmina from his holster and handed it up to Lydia.

"It's time I trusted you," he mumbled. "Can you use it?"

Lydia took the Luger in both hands almost as if it were some sort of an offering. She nodded.

Carter lay back on the pillow. Her figure was swimming above him.

"Sleep now," she said. "There will be no more battles. I will be here . . ."

It was dark. Carter lay nude on his stomach. He awoke to someone massaging his shoulder muscles with strong, sure fingers. He was aware that the entire day had passed, although he had no idea of the time.

"How do you feel?" Lydia asked above him, her voice soft, husky.

"What time is it?"

"About ten. You slept all day," Lydia said. She was straddling his hips. She got off, and he rolled over onto his back.

"No trouble?" he asked. He was stiff and still very sore, but he felt a lot better.

Lydia shook her head. Her long blond hair was down, and she was nude, the nipples of her large breasts erect. "It will come, though," she said. "I can feel it." She began gently massaging the muscles of his chest, her fingers lingering here and there around the various scars he had collected over the years.

Carter started to get up. He was hungry. After he had something to eat, he wanted to telephone Hawk, to see if Kobelev and Ganin had reacted to Borodin's death, and if another lure had surfaced. But Lydia pushed him back.

"Not yet," she said. She reached down and kissed his nipples, taking each between her lips and rolling her tongue around them.

The room was warm, but she was shivering. Carter could feel her entire body shaking. She was frightened.

He lifted her head, looked into her eyes for a long moment,

then she came into his arms and they kissed deeply, her mouth hot and demanding. He felt a sense of betrayal to Sigourney, but this was different; this was not love. It was nothing more than two people alone, comforting each other.

When they parted, Carter gently eased her over onto her back, kissed her chin, lingered at her neck, and then kissed her breasts.

She arched her back and moaned with pleasure, her shivering intensifying.

Carter stroked her thighs, her legs opening, and he worked his way down between her breasts to her navel, and to her hard, flat belly with his tongue. Her hips rose and fell, and her breath came faster.

She reached down and took his head in her hands, guiding him lower, between her legs. "Oh, God, it is wonderful," she murmured in Russian. "Please . . . please."

She was moist and ready. When Carter touched her with his tongue she jerked violently as if she had received an electric shock.

He raised his body and looked at her face. Her eyes were half closed, her lips parted.

"Yes?" she breathed. "Yes . . . now?"

Carter moved up, and she took him in her hands, guiding him inside her, her hips thrusting up to receive him, her legs coming up, locking around his back, her hands on his buttocks urging him against her.

He lingered, deep inside her for a long time, her hands up and down his back, and he kissed her breasts, taking the nipples in his mouth.

She moaned loudly, her entire body in barely controlled motion as Carter withdrew, then thrust within her again.

Slowly he made love to her, for the moment the terrible vision of Sigourney's body gone from his mind, lost in the comfort and pleasure of the here and now.

Lydia eased into the gentle motion with him, her pelvis

rising deliberately to meet his, her mouth open, her tongue flicking out, her eyes glazed.

They seemed to hang in a state of suspended time, their pleasure building by slow degrees.

Gone, too, from Carter's mind, for the moment, were thoughts about Kobelev and Ganin, and about the Russian he had killed that morning. Gone was his hunger and pain. All that was left was pleasure.

It went on for an eternity, higher and higher they went, until in the end they rose together in a blinding explosion, wave after wave of intense sensation that neither of them wanted ever to end.

When it was over, Carter lay back, and Lydia sat up to look down at his face. There was a sad expression in her eyes.

"It will never be like this again, will it," she said after a long time.

Carter smiled gently. "Nothing stays the same," he said.

"In the States . . ." she began.

"You will find someone." Carter answered her unspoken question.

The bedside telephone rang, shattering the fragile mood, and Carter sat up with a jerk. Lydia reared back, her hand to her mouth, her eyes wide.

The phone rang a second time. Carter picked it up.

"Yes?" he said.

"Are you rested, Mr. Carter?" a man's voice said in English, with a barely discernible Russian accent.

Carter got out of bed and took the phone with him to the window, the cord barely long enough to reach. There was a lot of traffic outside, but nothing suspicious.

"The maintenance van on the Avenue Montaigne," Carter said softly.

"Very perceptive of you," the Russian said.

"Arkadi Ganin."

Ganin laughed, the sound dry. "We think it terribly unfair

of you to have taken the girl. Nikolai is very angry.''

"The spoils of war," Carter replied. He motioned for Lydia to get dressed. "But you know where we are, why not come up here and get her?"

"It's not I who cares about the girl," Ganin said. "In any event, how do you suppose I found you?"

"You followed me. But you made a mistake."

"Yes?"

"You allowed me to rest. You should have come in for the kill directly after Borodin. Or was that poor old building employee too much for you?"

There was a very long silence on the line.

"What's the matter, Arkadi Konstantinovich? Has Kobelev pulled your leash up tight?" Carter taunted. "Tell me, has he had you kill the obligatory child yet? Are you good at that sort of thing? I understand it's Komodel's initiation rite."

Ganin did not rise to the bait. "I expected more from you than that, Carter. Much more. Perhaps Kobelev was exaggerating."

Lydia was pulling on her clothes. She had grabbed her suitcase and was throwing the rest of her things into it.

"What do you want?" Carter said.

"You."

"Not yet. Kobelev means to see me dead. I'm sure he wants to see me crawl on my hands and knees, but not here in Paris, not yet."

"Do not be so sure . . ."

"No, Kobelev's killing ground has already been set. Somewhere farther to the east. Finland, perhaps. Maybe Austria or Switzerland. Somewhere at risk to him, but a place I am sure to come. So, what do you want now?"

"As I said, Carter, you. But this time I'm going to give you a real chance at me. It is time, I think, that you and I meet."

"If and when I see you, I'll kill you, Ganin."

Ganin laughed. "You will *try*, Mr. Carter. That is all you can say for certain."

Carter grabbed his Luger from the nightstand, levered a round in the chamber while holding the telephone cradled on his shoulder, and slipped the weapon's safety off. Back by the window he looked outside.

"Show yourself," Carter snapped.

"Sure," Ganin said. "Across the street, second floor."

Carter looked across the street. A figure appeared in the window of a second-story apartment.

Ganin's laugh came over the phone. "I think it's time we meet, Mr. Carter. The Eiffel Tower, shall we say?"

"What time—" Carter began, but the connection was broken.

Carter threw the phone down and began pulling on his clothes. Ganin had found them at the hotel by following him that morning from Borodin's apartment. It meant there was a very good possibility that Kobelev's man did not know about the Jaguar sedan parked in the hotel's lot.

A plan was beginning to form in Carter's mind as he finished dressing and strapping on his weapons. Lydia was already by the door, so frightened she could barely keep still.

Hawk had also said that in order to beat Kobelev they'd have to play him at his own game.

It was foolish taking Ganin's challenge and meeting him that night, but it was the one thing Carter knew he was going to have to do. If he couldn't get a clear shot, at least the exercise would provide him, in some small measure, with an idea of just whom he was up against. Not some phantom figure on a computer printout, but a real flesh-and-blood person.

He grabbed his suitcase and opened the door a crack. The corridor was empty. He propelled Lydia out the door and down to the stairs as the elevator started up from the lobby.

Before they started down, Carter stood for a moment at the head of the stairs to listen. No one was there.

The elevator was just stopping at their floor when Carter and Lydia hit the stairs, taking them two at a time but making as little noise as possible.

At the bottom they turned right, going through a rear hallway, then out a side door to the small parking lot behind the hotel's outdoor garden area.

From there, beyond a tall stone fence, they could see the top of the Arc de Triomphe, illuminated against the night sky.

An older couple were just climbing out of a maroon Mercedes, and they looked up, startled, as Carter and Lydia raced to the Jaguar, unlocked it, and tossed their bags inside.

"Down!" Carter snapped as he started the powerful engine and swung around to the exit.

Lydia ducked down below window level as the Jaguar burst out onto the Rue de Berri, the tires skidding on the pavement as Carter hauled the wheel around. They shot up across St.-Honoré, then left to Avenue des Ternes.

Three blocks later Carter slowed down and began taking random turns left, then right, and right again, then left. Sometimes speeding up, sometimes slowing down. On the far side of the Bois de Boulogne he pulled over to the curb, doused the lights, and waited to see if they had been followed. But there was nothing other than the normal flow of traffic behind them. No vans, no cars, or anything else pulled up behind or ahead of them. They had made their break.

In the far distance, across the river, the Eiffel Tower rose above the city like some majestic rocket ship. Ganin wanted to meet him there. But when?

It was getting late. Nearly midnight. But Carter felt better than he had for a long time. A part of him cautioned against rising to Ganin's bait. Yet another inner voice told him he had no choice.

"I would like us to go now," Lydia said, breaking into his thoughts. "Back to London and then to the States."

Carter shook his head. "But we are leaving Paris tonight."

She brightened. "Now?"

"In a little while. Before morning."

She sagged again. "You are going off to meet him somewhere. What about me?"

"I'm going alone. You'll take the car and pick me up at exactly two o'clock."

"Where?"

"Along the Quai d'Orsay. Do you know it?"

"East of the Eiffel Tower."

"That's it. Come at two and again at two-thirty. But stop for no one or nothing else. Do you understand?"

She nodded. "And if you do not show up?"

"You're on your own. Get back to the States however you can and put an ad in the *Washington Post*: 'Nick's friend would like to meet with Smitty, care of the newspaper.' Someone will come for you."

"Like Kobelev?"

"Possibly. It'll be up to you," Carter said. He flipped on the headlights and pulled away from the curb.

"Don't do this thing, Nick," Lydia said.

Carter said nothing, and she looked away.

"I had to try," she said. "I'll be there. At two, and again at two-thirty."

Carter lit a cigarette, and they made their way through the fairly light traffic in silence for a while.

"This won't be over with tonight," he said at length.

"Perhaps it will be."

"Not unless he kills me, and I don't think he means to do that."

"Then why are you going to him?" Lydia almost screamed.

"To kill him," Carter said.

They drove the rest of the way in silence, all around the vast park, finally around to the Avenue de Versailles, which skirted the Seine on the opposite bank from the Eiffel Tower.

Near the Pont d'Iéna, which crossed the river directly in front of the tower, Carter pulled over, jumped out, and headed across on foot without looking back.

She would either be back at two or she wouldn't. Carter found that he didn't really care. Or at least he didn't at that moment.

For now his every thought went forward, to the upcoming confrontation. Just him and Ganin.

TEN

Despite the lateness of the hour, there were a number of people wandering around the base of the Eiffel Tower, including two lovers who sat down on one of the benches.

The tower itself was closed to the public for the night, and the restaurant on the first level was shut down, apparently for renovations.

Carter kept to one side of the broad promenade as he moved up to the base of the huge structure. He kept searching the shadows for a sign that Ganin was there, but he saw nothing. He looked up into the intricate latticework of the tower. Ganin wouldn't be down there waiting, Carter mused; he would be up top somewhere. Hiding in the darkness. It was logical.

A gendarme came up from the Champs de Mars and passed under the tower. Carter nodded, and the cop touched the brim of his cap.

On the far side of the base, Carter waited until the cop was out of sight, and then he quickly angled over to the southwest leg, where if he remembered correctly there was access to the stairs.

A large iron gate blocked the way. Looking around to make sure no one was watching, Carter pulled out his stiletto and started to pick the massive iron lock, but the latch came open in his hands.

The gate swung open, and Carter looked up. Ganin! The Russian had come this way and had left the gate open as an invitation.

Carter slipped Hugo back into its chamois sheath on his forearm, withdrew Wilhelmina, checked to make sure there was a round in the chamber and the safety was off, then stepped through the gate, closed and locked it behind him, and started up slowly, one step at a time into the darkness and whatever awaited him above.

Although he understood that Ganin would probably not make a serious try to kill him that night, he could not afford to take any chances. Whatever else the Russian assassin was, he definitely was not a fool. If a clear opportunity presented itself, he would not pass it up, no matter what Kobelev might have to say about it later. Carter's death, after all, was the entire reason for their elaborate scheme.

The huge structure angled inward toward the first level, mostly dark now that the restaurant was closed.

Near the head of the first run of iron stairs, Carter stopped. Below he could see the couples on the promenade, and on the river a *bâteau mouche* moved slowly under the bridge. He tried to pick out the gendarme but couldn't. The cop was either in the shadows or had moved back to the other side of the base.

Far above, the tower was bathed in lights, which threw crazy patterns within patterns on the gridwork structure. There were ten thousand places for an assassin to hide in waiting. Ten thousand places for the perfect ambush.

The tall iron gate blocking the first-level deck from the stairwell was ajar, just as the lower gate had been. Ganin had come this way. Again, an open invitation.

Carter eased the gate the rest of the way open, the thick hinges well oiled and noiseless.

Gripping his Luger tightly, and keeping low, Carter burst up onto the deck and rolled right then left, diving for the deeper shadows at the side of the enclosed structure as a single, silenced shot ricocheted off the metal rail less than a foot from where he had emerged from the stairwell.

It had come from above. There was no doubt of it.

Carter crouched there in the darkness, his every sense straining for a sound . . . any noise that would betray Ganin's location.

He heard it. Above. Far above. A chance scraping of shoe leather against an iron stair tread. Ganin was on the move. He was on his way up, which didn't make sense. At the top he would be cornered, unless he figured on using the elevator to come down while Carter was moving up the stairs. If that were the case, Ganin would be a sitting duck, an easy target as he passed Carter on the stairs.

An apparent mistake. But as far as Carter knew, the Russian did not make mistakes.

He worked his way along the restaurant wall to the center, where again the gate to the stairwell had been left ajar.

For a long moment he stared at the open gate, but then he turned and went back toward the core of the tower. Around the corner he found the electrical panels behind a wire cage. Heavy cables ran to the elevator motors.

Holstering Wilhelmina, Carter withdrew Hugo, and within sixty seconds he had the cage open and was inside.

Signs in several languages were posted all over the place, warning of the high voltage.

In the semidarkness Carter studied the layout for a minute or so, finally opening one of the large panels. Inside were two massive switches marked ELEVATOR MAIN POWER.

Carter gingerly reached out and pulled both switches to the off position. Then he closed the panel, stepped back out of the cage, and relocked the door.

He glanced up. Whatever happened now, Ganin would not be taking the elevator down. Carter could now be sure that the Russian would be stuck on top.

Yet even as Carter thought it, and as he moved silently back to the stairs and started up, he wondered if the solution hadn't been too simple. Would a man such as Ganin have overlooked the obvious? Or did he mean to force the issue, despite his protestations on the telephone to the contrary? Perhaps this was the killing ground after all. Perhaps only one of them would be coming down. . . .

The stairs zigzagged their way up the center of the tower in tight little patterns. At each switchback, Carter stopped to search the gridwork above and to listen for any further chance sounds, but all was quiet.

As he climbed, all of Paris began to spread out beneath him. In the far distance across the river he could see the Sacré Coeur, lit up on its hill, looking lovely and peaceful.

Another silenced shot whined off the iron rail near where Carter stood, this time so close it sent paint chips flying into his face.

Moments later Carter could hear the distinctive ring of shoe leather on the metal treads, moving upward.

He was less than a hundred feet from the top. He raced up the next few flights relying on his speed of motion, rather than the darkness and his stealth, for safety.

Two more shots ricocheted off the metalwork, until within thirty or forty feet of the top he spotted a figure moving on the catwalk.

Carter snapped off a shot, his unsilenced Luger extremely loud in the night air, and the figure disappeared.

The stairs were covered from above. There was no way he would be able to make it the rest of the way. . . .

Again Carter holstered Wilhelmina, then he climbed up onto the rail and swung out over to the gridwork of the tower, the sheer drop more than eight hundred feet to the deck of the first level.

The metal was slippery with night dew, the corners rounded and at odd, oblique angles, making any kind of grip or foothold extremely difficult.

Carter worked his way around to the outside of the tower, the place Ganin would least expect him to be, and started up, the wind at that height moaning through the gridwork, threatening to dislodge his grip and send him plunging far below to the pavement.

He concentrated on each handhold, on each step upward, a few inches at a time, his world reduced for the moment to hanging on.

Within ten feet of the top, Carter stopped a moment to rest, to gather his strength. His wounded leg was starting to give him some trouble again. He had put too much strain on it during the past few days, but there was no going back now, so he put it out of his mind.

A few feet farther up he heard the clinking of what sounded like thin metal tubing hitting the tower's metalwork, and then a soft slapping sound . . . almost like a sail.

Suddenly it was clear to him. Ganin had not made a mistake after all.

Redoubling his efforts, Carter scrambled recklessly the last few feet to the base of the observation room, then climbed through the gridwork to the stairs.

He pulled out his Luger, thumbed the safety off, and cautiously came up through the doorway.

Arkadi Ganin, a large hang glider, its nylon wing black, strapped to his back, stood perched in precarious balance above on the observation room's roof.

Carter fired a shot through the open trapdoor just as the Russian launched himself and was gone.

A large satchel stood in the middle of the observation room. Carter started up to the roof, when he noticed it out of the corner of his eye. His stomach flopped over, and he scrambled back down.

The satchel was locked, but from within Carter was certain he could smell the distinctive odor of vinegar. It was an acid fuse. Activated. There was a bomb inside!

He whipped out his stiletto and, working with extreme care, slit open the leather side of the squat briefcase. It was possible the lock was tied to an override switch.

Easing open the flap he had cut, he looked inside. Through a tubular fuse the size of a pencil, wires connected two batteries to a thick lump of pastique. Enough to blow the entire tower.

Sweat pouring down his chest beneath his shirt, Carter reached inside the case with his right hand, grabbed the slender fuse between his thumb and forefinger, took a deep breath, and yanked the device out of the plastique. A split second later the fuse sputtered, and a long, deadly-looking spark emerged from the business end.

Carter fell back on his haunches and breathed a deep sigh of relief. Ganin had cut it very close. To within a few seconds. Had Carter gone up on the roof for another shot, he would not have survived.

Yet he didn't think the Russian really wanted him dead. Not yet. This had been just another test to see how good he was.

Carter was certain now of one crucial fact: Ganin was very good. A hell of a lot better than any of them had given him credit for being.

A minute or so later Carter got to his feet and climbed up to the roof of the observation room. He looked out over the city. There was no sign of Ganin with the hang glider, of course, but he found what he was looking for on the roof. Blood. Not much of it, but he didn't need much to know. He had hit Ganin. It would make the Russian think twice about playing his little games.

● ● ●

Apparently because of the height above the ground, no one below had heard either of Carter's two shots. It was already a few minutes after two by the time he made it painfully back down to the gate in the southwest leg, unlocked it, and stepped away from the tower.

The strolling couples were gone, as were the lovers on the bench. Carter hurried up the Quai Branly, past where the tour boats landed and departed, to the Quai d'Orsay where he hoped Lydia would be making her second swing in the next few minutes.

As he walked he continued to scan possible places of ambush. While Ganin had him occupied, he suspected that someone had gone to the hotel in an effort to get Lydia. When they found her gone, they'd have to figure she was somewhere near Carter.

A lot depended, of course, on whether or not they knew about the Jaguar yet, and whether or not Lydia had kept her head during the past two hours. If she had been spotted, they might have managed to stop her.

Carter got to the Quai Branly where it intersected with the Avenue Bosquet at the Pont de l'Alma just before two-thirty, and he sat down on one of the benches that faced the Seine.

An occasional car passed, then a truck, before the Jaguar came roaring across the bridge, its headlights flashing on Carter.

He jumped up as the car screeched around the corner and pulled up to the curb.

Lydia slid over to the passenger side as Carter jumped in behind the wheel, slammed the car in gear, and took off, the tires squealing on the dry pavement.

Lydia was frightened out of her mind. Even in the dark interior of the car, Carter could see that she was pale, her eyes wide and moist.

As he drove he kept glancing up into the rearview mirror to make sure they weren't being followed.

"They're after you, Nick," Lydia sputtered as they crossed the river near the French Naitonal Assembly Building.

"Yes, Ganin and Kobelev," Carter snapped.

"No, listen to me!" she cried. "The French police are after you. It was on the radio."

They had picked up a tail, the headlights coming around the corner from the bridge, following them up to the Place de la Concorde.

"What are you talking about?" Carter asked, concentrating more on his driving. He hauled the car around a tight corner, and a block later swung left, nearly running up on the curb.

Lydia looked back. "They're following us?"

"Hang on tight," Carter said as they squealed around still another corner.

For the next few minutes Carter put the powerful Jag through its paces, running an intricate random pattern through the early-morning streets until, way out on the Rue de Flandre heading for the E2 highway east to Reims, he was satisfied they had lost their tail.

He turned back to Lydia. "Now, what did you say about the French police?"

"Listen to me—they have your description. They say you murdered a French maintenance man in Borodin's building, as well as Borodin himself, whom they're describing as an important Soviet journalist."

Carter managed a slight smile. It was Kobelev's signal again. But there had to be more.

"What in God's name are you laughing about?" Lydia shrieked. "If the French arrest you, and put you in jail, Ganin will be able to get to you with no problem! You'll be as good as dead if you're arrested!"

"What else?" he asked.

"What are you talking about?"

"What else?" Carter repeated. "There was something else in the news story. You listened to the entire thing?"

Lydia nodded. ''They said you entered the building, killed the Frenchman, and then went upstairs and broke Borodin's neck. The Soviet government has launched a protest—naturally—and called you a capitalist hoodlum of the worst kind. They want immediate justice.''

''There's more,'' Carter insisted.

Lydia shook her head in frustration. ''There's nothing—'' she started, but then she stopped in mid-sentence. ''But—''

''What is it?''

''It's Bonn, West Germany. Kobelev wants you to go there.''

''How do you know that?''

''It was on the radio. They said Borodin was to have gone to Bonn next week. A new assignment.''

Was the killing ground to be in Bonn? Carter wondered. They were coming much closer now to the Iron Curtain. It was only a few hours by car from Bonn—much less by helicopter—to East Germany and complete safety for Kobelev.

For some inexplicable reason, though, Carter did not think Bonn was the final destination. There would be more; he was willing to bet on it. Paris was a close call. Kobelev would want him to squirm some more, especially since Ganin, his star pupil, had been wounded. And because Lydia was still on the loose.

The tolerances in Bonn would be much closer. Bonn was going to be a dangerous experience for them all. Kobelev was angry about Lydia. Ganin would be angry that he had allowed himself to be wounded. The French police, and therefore Interpol, would be after Carter. And Lydia was desperately frightened. Bonn would be difficult.

There was very little traffic at this hour of the morning, mostly large transport trucks on the superhighway.

Carter lit a cigarette as he sped up, his mind working out the possibilities in Bonn. He was going to need a bit more information, as well as some help now from Hawk. He did not want a confrontation at the frontier with the French police. He would not allow himself to be arrested, of course, but if there was an incident at the border, it would be a clear signal to Kobelev and Ganin just where he was.

They passed through Reims at about four in the morning, then continued east through Verdun, and finally into Metz, about thirty miles from the West German border.

They got off the A1 and went into the city, where Carter circled around the central railway station several times before he headed to the far side of the town.

"What is it?" Lydia asked. "What are you doing?"

Carter pulled up at a long-term parking area. The night shift attendant was getting set to go off duty, but he took Carter's payment in advance, issued a card, and then took the car.

With their suitcases in hand, Carter and Lydia started away from the parking lot on foot, heading back into the city's center.

"Ganin knows about the car now. As soon as we come into Bonn they'll spot us," Carter said.

Lydia stopped. Carter turned back.

"We're going to Bonn? After Paris, you still want to go to Bonn? What about the police?"

"I'll take care of it."

She looked back. "What about the car?"

"Someone will be picking it up. For now, we're going by train."

Lydia shook her head. "What if I tell you I want to get off this merry-go-round right now?"

"That's fine," Carter said. "I'll have you met at Dulles in Washington by someone you can trust." He turned and continued walking downtown, spotting a cab just across the street.

He didn't bother looking back as he crossed over to the

taxi, but he knew that she was behind him, and he held the door for her.

She climbed in, a scowl on her face, but she said nothing.

"The train station," Carter said.

A few minutes later they were deposited outside the ornate old station. Carter paid the driver, and he and Lydia went inside where they bought first-class tickets, with their own private compartment, on the train to Bonn, which went to Luxembourg first, then Koblenz before arriving in Bonn at about one in the afternoon, the trip made longer because of the two stops. It left at eight-thirty, which gave them plenty of time to have some breakfast in the station's café. First Carter went to one of the telephone kiosks and placed a call to Hawk's Washington number.

It was just a bit after one in the morning in Washington, but Hawk answered his phone on the first ring.

"I'm in Metz," Carter said. He glanced up. Lydia had gone across the main hall to the newsstand where she was purchasing a newspaper.

"What happened in Paris?" Hawk demanded.

Quickly and succinctly, Carter went over everything that had happened from the moment he and Lydia had arrived at the Lancaster until they got to Metz, leaving nothing out, including the speculation that Bonn itself would probably not be his final destination.

"What are your plans for Bonn? Have you got another of Kobelev's people picked out?"

"No, sir. I was hoping you would have some information. Something must be happening in Bonn at the moment. Kobelev sent me the signal . . . Bonn was where Borodin was supposedly being reassigned. What else is happening there now?"

"Not a thing, Nick," Hawk said. "Nothing has been on the overnight report except that the French want you for questioning in Borodin's murder."

"Are you sure?"

"Of course."

It didn't make sense. Kobelev was obviously luring him to Bonn, but for what purpose? Unless it was too soon? Unless they were waiting until he showed up. . . .

Lydia came back to the phone kiosk with a newspaper. She held it up for Carter to see. His photograph was on the front page, under the headline THIS MAN WANTED FOR MURDER.

"I made the front page," Carter told Hawk.

"When does your train leave?" Hawk asked.

"Eight-thirty, local."

"I'll call Bradley at State. We'll work something out with the French authorities before you reach the border this morning."

"I don't want to get into anything with the French police."

"Of course not. Kobelev and Ganin would love for it to happen, though."

"Yes, sir."

"How is the woman holding up?"

"Reasonably well, although I don't know how much longer it will last. They want her pretty badly.'

"Be careful, Nick," Hawk said. "Whatever they've got planned for you in Bonn will not be very pleasant."

"Yes, sir," Carter said. "But I don't think it'll be very long now before the final confrontation will come."

ELEVEN

It was a few minutes after noon when the Soviet jet transport landed at the military airstrip in Marzahn on the outskirts of East Berlin. It had come on a direct flight from Moscow. Normally there would have been a lot of military fanfare, but this time only a limousine was waiting. The big car raced out to the transport, which had taxied to a stop in an isolated parking area.

The aircraft's door popped open, boarding stairs were brought up, and Nikolai Fedor Kobelev, dressed in civilian clothes, stepped down to the tarmac. He was alone, and he looked very angry.

He strode across to the limo as the driver leaped out, raced around to the rear door, and opened it.

"Welcome to Berlin, comrade . . ." the driver started, but the look on Kobelev's face stopped him in mid-sentence.

Kobelev climbed into the car. Arkadi Ganin sat on the opposite side, his eyes hollow, his complexion somewhat pale.

"Comrade General," Ganin said softly. There was no fear in his eyes, something Kobelev had been concerned about.

"How did this happen?" Kobelev barked.

The driver had gotten in behind the wheel, and they moved off the airstrip.

"He came up the outside of the tower," Ganin said. "It was incredible. I looked down, and there he was."

"Had your silly bomb gone off . . . *then* what, Arkadi Konstantinovich? Or had Carter been a split second earlier—and his shot done more than simply give you a flesh wound—then what?"

"It did not happen, comrade. And now he is wanted by the police—"

"Already their State Department has calmed the French, who are claiming they were looking for the wrong man," Kobelev cut in.

Ganin sat forward in surprise.

"Yes, Nick Carter has his own 'puppet master.' David Hawk. He is very good. He has caused me trouble before."

"Eliminate him."

"Impossible, let me tell you."

Ganin sank back in the seat. "Where is Carter now?"

"Presumably on his way to Bonn, although he has not yet been spotted. But our people there will find him."

Ganin kept silent.

"And when they do, you will leave him alone," Kobelev said with feeling. "You will not go to Bonn."

"I do not understand . . ."

"No, you do not!" Kobelev exploded. "In Paris your simple job was to get the girl. You were to have lured Carter out of his hotel, and then gone in for her. There would have been time later for you to meet with him. Your little trick nearly cost us the entire operation. You badly underestimated Carter. The next time he will kill you. And if he does not, I will."

Ganin, chastised, said nothing. There was nothing he could say. Kobelev was an awesome power in Moscow. An angry Kobelev was ten thousand times more dangerous.

Kobelev forced himself to calm down. He had done a lot of thinking about this problem on the flight from Moscow, and he had come to a number of conclusions. More than ever before he wanted Carter dead. Only now he realized he had gone at the assignment with blinders on. He had gone ahead forgetting just how dangerous Carter and his boss, David Hawk, were.

There would be no more playing around. He would dislodge Carter from Bonn as soon as possible and either recapture or kill the girl. And, in the end, he would make sure Carter was killed. At the very first opportunity, no matter how crude, how abrupt, or how messy it was. There would be no more games with N3. He was going to be a dead man the moment he stepped outside of Bonn.

There were too many delicate operations going on in Bonn at the moment, with the regular KBG, to go after Carter there. It would upset the Presidium. He had been told that, in no uncertain terms, just before he had left Moscow: "Wrap this up, Comrade General. Soon, but not in Bonn. There can be no involvement by yourself or Ganin in Bonn."

Kobelev turned to Ganin.

"Tonight you will go and make sure everything is in readiness," he said. "There will be no mistakes this time. The moment he steps into your sights, I want him dead."

A hard look had come into Ganin's eyes. He nodded. "It is a change in plans, then, Comrade General? I am to kill him at the first opportunity?"

"At the very first opportunity!"

"And the girl?"

Kobelev smiled. "The girl will be taken care of in Bonn. Rest assured."

It was cold, overcast, and raining when the train from Metz pulled into the station in downtown Bonn. There had been no trouble at the border crossings, nor were there any delays in the West German capital.

Outside the station they got a cab, and Carter ordered the driver to take them out to the Köln-Bonn airport a few miles northwest of the city. Lydia was surprised, but she said nothing.

It bothered Carter that beyond the announcement of Borodin's pending ''assignment'' to Bonn, Kobelev had done nothing else to spotlight this as the next location.

There was the possibility that Ganin's wound was severe enough to take him out of the picture. In that case the puppet master would be regrouping somewhere. Rethinking his next objective. But Carter doubted that was the case. There had not been enough blood on the roof of the observation room. Carter was betting that Ganin's wound was nothing more than a superficial one.

Kobelev's real concern at the moment, he suspected, would be Lydia's continued freedom. Perhaps they were going to use Bonn as nothing more than the place where they'd attempt to get her back. Or kill her.

He glanced at her. She was very frightened. She was not a stupid woman. Most likely she had come to the same conclusion herself. Now Carter wanted to buy them an escape hole before they were spotted in Bonn, which he had no doubt they would be. In fact he *wanted* to be spotted by Kobelev's people. Perhaps it would force their hand.

At the airport an hour later, Carter bought two first-class tickets—Bonn to Frankfurt, then Frankfurt direct to New York—under their cover names on the flight that left the following morning at eight o'clock.

At first Lydia thought they were actually going back to the States, but in the café where they had a late lunch, he dashed her hopes.

''They'll know we're here by this afternoon at the latest,'' he said.

"So we keep under cover until morning, and then leave?" she inquired hopefully.

Carter shook his head. "Kobelev hasn't set up anything here in Bonn for us. He'll know we're here. I'm merely forcing his hand. He'll know about our reservations, which will give him until eight tomorrow morning to do something."

Lydia looked at him incredulously. "You love this, don't you?"

"It's my job," Carter said flatly. "Before it's over, Ganin and Kobelev will be dead."

"Either that, or you and I will be dead," she said softly. She raised her head. "I don't want to play this game any longer."

"You have no choice now."

Lydia sucked in her breath and lowered her eyes. "I was afraid you were going to say that."

"Until he's dead, he won't rest with you out there on the loose. You know that."

She nodded. "I know."

"There will be an attempt here in Bonn to grab you."

"Or kill me," she said.

Carter nodded. At this stage of the game nothing would be gained by lying to her. "I'm going to make sure that doesn't happen."

Another thought dawned on her. "My God, you're going to use me as bait!"

"You're as safe here, Lydia, as you would be anywhere else. At least here we have a fair idea of what to expect. With the reservations for the flight tomorrow morning, we even know the time frame. It'll force Kobelev's hand. Whatever happens here will lead to him and to Ganin. And then it will truly be finished. Once and for all you will be free without fear of reprisal."

"They'll keep coming after me."

"No. Once Kobelev is dead, the Kremlin will want no further part of this thing. They'll back off, lick their wounds, and try something different somewhere else. Once Kobelev and Ganin are eliminated, the book will be closed."

"I wish I could believe that."

"Believe it, Lydia, because there is nothing else."

They rented a Mercedes 190, a small sedan, at the Hertz counter and drove back into Bonn, checking in at the Königshof Hotel on Adenauerallee just off the Münsterplatz in the heart of the downtown area. It was a fine old hotel with a good wine cellar and a particularly good restaurant. Carter picked the hotel because it was a favorite for visiting businessmen, and it would be a place where he and Lydia would be fairly visible.

They could do nothing until Kobelev made his next move, which would not happen if they went deep.

After they cleaned up and changed they went down to the bar, where they had a couple of drinks, and then went into the dining room for an excellent dinner.

"When this is over I'd like to live in New York. Manhattan," Lydia said over coffee.

"Why is that?" Carter asked, smiling.

"It is an exciting city. Like Moscow, only a lot brighter. There are many places there for me to work. I could be a translator."

"Perhaps we will offer you a job."

Lydia was startled. "You mean with the CIA or something?"

"Or something."

She shook her head. "No. When this is over I think I will have had enough of that sort of business. You must remember I was raised on this sort of thing, living in the Soviet Union."

"I understand," Carter said, and he did. "Whatever it is you want, we'll help you with it. I promise."

She looked deeply into his eyes. For the first time in twenty-four hours, she didn't seem to be in abject terror. "You are a good man, Nick Carter, even though you have a blind spot concerning Nikolai Fedor."

Carter's jaw tightened. "He's a ruthless, dangerous man."

She agreed. "And so are you, I think."

Carter lit a cigarette and looked away. Sigourney seemed so terribly far away. It scared him to think how fast her memory was fading.

The waiter brought their check, Carter paid it, and he and Lydia went outside, across toward the university. The rain had let up for the moment, although it was bitterly cold. Traffic was light. Carter paid very strict attention to every car or truck or van that passed them. Something would come, perhaps early this evening. More likely in the middle of the night.

They took a turn through the university grounds, but then Lydia became cold, and she asked if they couldn't return to the hotel.

"What happens if he makes no move between now and eight in the morning?" she asked on the way back.

"That's not likely."

"Tonight, then?"

Carter nodded. The same blue Ford Cortina that had passed them on their way up from the hotel drifted slowly by. There were two men in the car. Carter managed to get a fairly good look at both of them as the car passed beneath a streetlight. Neither of them was Ganin; of that he was absolutely certain. In fact neither of them had looked like Russian KGB.

The hotel doorman opened the double glass doors for them, and they crossed the lobby and took the elevator up. Something didn't feel right to Carter, so he punched the button for the second floor, and they got off there.

Carter and Lydia watched from an alcove around the corner from the main ballroom as the elevator continued up to the eighth floor, then was recalled to the lobby.

The car stayed on the ground floor for half a minute, then started up. Carter reached inside his jacket for his Luger to make sure it was ready.

The elevator doors opened, and two husky men, guns drawn, stepped out. Another two inside the elevator continued up.

There was no doubt in the Killmaster's mind who and what they were after, but they just didn't look like Russians to Carter, and that bothered him. Who the hell were they?''

Carter turned, and holding Lydia by the elbow, he hustled her silently down the corridor, into the ballroom, and across the dance floor to the rear exits, where they took the back stairs two at a time.

At the bottom they ducked through the kitchen, through the loading dock area, and out the back way, pulling up short as a pair of headlights turned the corner into the alley and came their way.

There would be someone out front, Carter supposed, as well as this car, and the four men upstairs.

They turned and hurried back through the loading dock and supply area, where at the rear they found a heavy steel door that opened onto a set of stairs that led down into the darkness.

Carter found the light switch and flipped it on, and they headed down into the bowels of the hotel where he supposed the heating plant was located, and which contained the plumbing and sewage lines.

This was a service entrance. At the bottom of the stairs they found themselves in a long tunnel lined with a maze of pipes, some of them wrapped in asbestos cloth, some equipped with huge valves.

Lights were strung at fifty-foot intervals down the long

tunnel, which ran parallel with the street and apparently ran at least the length of the block beneath all the buildings above.

Carter and Lydia hurried along the tunnel, their heels echoing in the narrow confines, until they came to another stairwell up.

The stairwell door at the hotel, back the way they had just come, clattered. Careful not to grab hold of a live steam pipe, Carter quickly scrambled up the pipes along the wall, pulled out his stiletto, and at the top reached out and cut through the electrical wires connecting all the tunnel lights.

There were several large sparks, and the tunnel was suddenly plunged into darkness.

Carter jumped down, groped for and found Lydia, and the two of them made their way to the stairwell and softly went up.

At the top, Carter listened at the door. There were no sounds from the other side, although he could hear someone coming down the tunnel behind them.

Unlatching the steel door, Carter eased it open onto a plain corridor with cement walls. No one was there.

He and Lydia slipped out into the corridor, then rushed to the back door, which opened onto the same alley as the hotel, but up a hundred yards, and around a slight bend.

They slipped outside, and keeping an eye on the alley for any pursuers, they walked up to the street, then turned right toward the river.

"They were not Russians," Lydia said breathlessly.

"Are you sure?"

"Of course I'm sure!" she snapped. "What the hell is going on?"

Carter glanced back over his shoulder, but no one was coming after them. They had made a clean break. "I don't know. But I'm going to find out."

They walked up toward the Kennedy Bridge, and a couple of blocks later, Carter hailed a passing cab. He ordered the driver to take them to a small hotel near the railway station. Once, many years ago, he had stayed there. It was one of the lesser establishments in Bonn, and the clerks asked no questions.

The cabby smiled smugly, sure that he was bringing a couple to an illicit rendezvous.

He dropped them off in front of the seedy hotel, and Carter tipped him well.

Inside, the clerk grinned as Carter rented the room under the name Herr Schmidt, and upstairs Carter made sure Lydia understood where the fire escape was located so that if the need arose she had a bolt-hole.

"We're leaving first thing in the morning, no matter what does or doesn't happen," Carter said.

Lydia's eyes were wide. She looked up at him. "And if you don't come for me . . .?"

"I will," Carter said with more confidence than he actually felt. Kobelev had been ahead of them all the way. "Seven o'clock sharp, I'll pick you up in front of the train station."

"In the Mercedes?"

Carter nodded. "But listen to me, Lydia," he said. "No matter what happens, *no matter what*, stay here. Don't leave the room for anyone or anything until morning."

She nodded.

For a moment a twinge of real fear and guilt crossed his mind. The instructions he was giving her were much the same as the fatal instructions he had given to Sigourney a thousand years ago.

"What is it?" Lydia asked, reading something of that in his eyes.

"Just stay here until morning. I'll see you at seven."

She nodded again, and Carter turned and left the room.

It had started to drizzle again. Carter pulled up his coat collar and walked over to the station, where he got a cab that took him across town to within a block of the Köngishof Hotel. He went the rest of the way on foot.

The desk clerk looked up in surprise as Carter walked into the lobby, but then he smiled and nodded.

Something was up. But it was something that the desk clerk knew about. Carter doubted that Kobelev would be so open about stalking him, so it meant something else was in store.

He took the elevator to the eighth floor and walked down the corridor to their room. He opened the door and stepped inside, directly into two husky men with drawn pistols.

He stopped short and slowly raised his hands. These were not Russians. They were definitely not Russians.

A third man, dressed in a plain dark suit, came around the corner and frisked Carter, coming up only with Wilhelmina. He looked at the Luger, shook his head, and pocketed it.

"Where is she?" he said in English.

"Who?" Carter replied. The man was German. Obviously a cop.

"The woman you checked in with."

"Her."

"Yes, Mr. Scott. Your wife. Elizabeth Scott . . . also known as Lydia Borasova."

"Never heard of her," Carter said. Kobelev had done his work well.

"She is wanted for the murder of a Soviet diplomat in New York City. Petr Lashkin. They were lovers. Were you aware of that?"

Carter said nothing.

The German patted Carter's Luger in his coat pocket. "Have you any idea of the penalty in West Germany for carrying a concealed weapon? An unregistered concealed weapon?"

"I am sorry, Herr . . ." Carter said.

"My name is of no importance. Only your name is. And I

am sure it is not Scott. Would you care to enlighten me?''

"If I gave you a telephone number, Officer—a number that would clear up any questions you might have—would you call it?''

The German cop stared at Carter, a very hard expression in his eyes. Finally he shook his head and stepped a little closer. "I think not. You know, I believe you are a spy. Perhaps for the Russians, since you are traveling with a Russian murderess . . . whom we will find, by the way.'' He shook his head again. "No, I think I would rather have the chance to talk with you. Just you and me, you know, for a day or two. Perhaps longer. However long it takes.''

The other two cops heard none of that.

The German cop pulled Carter's Luger out of his pocket and examined it closely this time. He looked up. "An interesting weapon,'' he said. "No serial numbers.''

"How much has the KGB paid you to help out, comrade?'' Carter asked quietly.

A flinty expression came into the German's eyes the moment before he stepped forward and swung.

Carter feinted back, blocked the punch, and hit the cop with every ounce of his strength in the solar plexus.

The man grunted once and went to his knees.

The other two leaped forward as Carter grabbed Wilhelmina, then the Killmaster jumped back and slammed the door in their faces.

He spun around and raced down the corridor toward the stairs. Kobelev was good. Damned good. But now, at last, Carter felt he was beginning to have the man's measure.

TWELVE

The elevator was still on the eighth floor. Carter reached inside, punched the button for the lobby, then continued down the corridor to the stairwell.

Just inside the door he waited for a moment as the two German cops skidded around the corner. They looked up at the elevator indicator, then one of them pulled out a walkie-talkie. They had someone in the lobby, just as Carter had thought they might.

He turned and hurried down the stairs, taking them recklessly two and three at a time.

At the bottom he holstered Wilhelmina, straightened his jacket, and stepped out into the main corridor where he headed across to the lobby.

The desk clerk spotted him halfway to the front doors, but he was so stunned for several crucial seconds that he said and did nothing.

Two cops waited by the elevator, which was just opening as Carter made it to the front doors. The clerk came alive at that moment, shouting and gesturing toward the door.

The doorman suddenly stepped up. Carter stiff-armed the

big man, stumbling and nearly falling in the process, then raced across the street, down the block, and into the university grounds, the sounds of whistles and distant sirens beginning to fill the night.

Because of the hour—it was a few minutes after ten—and the weather, the university was deserted. Carter followed the sidewalks through the trees and gardens, passing ornate baroque buildings and statues, finally emerging on the other side of the complex.

The huge cathedral on Münsterplatz rose up tall in the misty night sky, as did the town hall building just beyond it.

He managed to make it across the broad street and down a narrow avenue that led over to another main thoroughfare just as a police car, its blue lights flashing, its siren blaring, screamed around from Adenauerallee.

Carter ducked into the shadows of a shop doorway as the police car passed, then he hurried across the main avenue and down another side street.

It took him nearly forty minutes to make it to the hotel near the railroad station where he had left Lydia.

There were no suspicious-looking characters outside, and no police were there—yet. Nevertheless, Carter went around to the back of the hotel, pulled down the fire-escape ladder, and scrambled up to their third-floor room.

The curtains were half open, the room in darkness. But Carter could see that no one was inside. Lydia was gone.

The window was unlocked. He shoved it open and climbed inside. Closing the curtains, he flipped on the lights.

The room was empty. A chair by the writing desk was turned over, as was the wastepaper basket.

Lydia was gone. The German police had been nothing more than a diversion to keep Carter busy. It meant that they had been spotted by Kobelev's people, had been followed here to this hotel, and once Carter left they had grabbed the woman.

It was the same business that was used on St. Anne's. Sigourney had been killed during a similar scenario. *Christ! The same damned pattern*, Carter thought. First, Kobelev created a signal that caused Carter to come running. Next, he engineered a diversion. And in the end—in the Caribbean, in New York, in Paris, and now in Bonn—Kobelev had his way.

In frustration, Carter took the small room apart piece by piece, looking for something—anything—that Lydia might have left behind. Any kind of a sign or clue as to what had happened there. But he found nothing.

He stood, finally, by the window looking out. Kobelev's tactics were as simple as they were sophisticated.

First the unmistakable flag, and then the diversion.

It was the puppet master's game. It was time now, Carter decided, to play the man at his own pace. He had invented the rules; Carter would now use them. And with a vengeance.

He made sure the room was neat and tidy, then he slipped out the window, down the fire escape, and around the corner to the train station.

The last train out for the evening would be departing in a few minutes, at midnight, for Munich, which was exactly where Carter wanted to go.

Kobelev would not want him stopped in Bonn, so he was certain the police had not been tipped off about the run-down hotel. The police had been nothing more than a means of prying Lydia loose from Carter's grasp.

He only hoped that Kobelev had not yet had her killed. He suspected the Russian would ultimately use her as the bait for the final confrontation.

Carter bought a one-way ticket, first-class, boarded the train, and exactly at midnight it pulled out of the now nearly deserted station and headed east back through the city, before turning south for the eight-hour run to the capital city of Bavaria.

He settled back, alone in the compartment, the lights out as he watched the countryside slip by. He was nearly a hundred-percent certain that remaining in Bonn would have accomplished nothing for him. If Ganin had ever been there, which he seriously doubted, he would be gone by now. Lydia would be gone as well.

They would all be heading to wherever the killing ground was located. The final confrontation would come very soon, only Kobelev was in for a nasty surprise before it happened.

The train stopped in Frankfurt for twenty minutes a few hours later. Carter cautiously got off and went upstairs to the vast terminal, at the early hour nearly deserted except for the maintenance crew.

At one of the telephone kiosks he placed a credit card call to Smitty in Washington, D.C., and before the Operations chief could make any objections, Carter passed on some hurried instructions and hung up.

From vending machines Carter bought a couple of beers and a sandwich, then reboarded the train. A few minutes later it pulled out of the station for the long haul down to Mannheim, Stuttgart, Augsburg, and finally Munich.

After he ate, he managed to get some sleep until the cold dawn broke gray over the German countryside. In the small pull-down sink in his compartment, Carter splashed some water on his face, then rang the porter for coffee and the morning newspapers.

There was no mention in the Frankfurt newspaper about the incident in Bonn, but then Carter would have been surprised had there been anything. He searched for something else in the newspaper's international section, finally spotting what he took to be a possibility. An American NATO adviser and his wife, whose first name was listed in the paper as Lydia, were killed when an avalanche suddenly roared down over a high pass road sweeping their car over the edge. One witness reported hearing a large bang, such as the noise an avalanche cannon might make. The report, however, had so far been unconfirmed.

The incident occurred late yesterday near Innsbruck, the Austrian skiing town barely a hundred miles south of Munich.

Carter put the paper down. If the Innsbruck mention were another Kobelev flag, and he expected it was, the puppet master would be expecting him to make his way there immediately.

Carter smiled inwardly, his eyes hard and cold. He would go to Innsbruck, all right. But not right away. First he was going to strike back in Munich. He was going to draw Ganin back into Germany. He'd play them at their own game.

It was raining and gusting in Munich when Carter got off the train and stepped outside the ornate railway station. Charlie Mann, his AXE contact in Munich, was waiting at the curb in a battered BMW sedan.

Carter crossed the broad sidewalk and climbed into the car. Immediately Mann pulled away from the curb and headed past the Frauenkirche, the twin church towers symbolizing the city.

"All hell has been breaking loose overnight," Mann said.

"Anything from Bonn?"

Mann nodded. "Hawk's been on the horn with the head of the German Federal Police. They want you pretty badly. Seems you roughed up one of their top cops."

"Anything happening here in Munich?" Carter asked.

"Not a thing, although I suspect that's about to change."

"Not until I have a shower and a shave. Did you bring the things I asked for?"

Mann nodded over his shoulder toward the back seat. "In the leather bag. The Bonn police have your things impounded, including a very curious cassette recorder with an unusual circuit board arrangement.''

Carter used the recorder to transport his weapons through airline security systems. If the police had taken it apart, they'd know what it had been used for. It meant they'd know he was armed with more than the Luger.

They drove in silence for the next few minutes. Mann had circled the central downtown area twice before he headed up the Schützenstrasse, very near the railway station they had just left.

"I've got you booked at the Excelsior—not the best in town but certainly not the worst. It's quiet."

"Have you got my passport?" Carter asked.

Again Mann looked at him. "It was the one thing that made Smitty nervous."

Carter said nothing.

"The Bonn police have your Scott passport, but Smitty couldn't understand why you wanted a passport in your own name. It'll be like a big neon sign for the opposition."

Carter nodded. "Exactly."

"I see," Mann said. "Are you going to need some help here in town?"

"Only under two conditions, Charlie. The first is that you do exactly as I tell you. No questions."

Mann nodded. "And the second?"

"No matter what happens afterward, you make no attempt to follow me or to offer any further assistance."

Again Mann nodded. They pulled up to the hotel. "What's the target?"

"The Soviet compound," Carter said. "I want to light a little fire under them tonight."

Mann whistled. "All hell is going to break loose, not only with the Russians but with the German police."

"I hope so," Carter said. "I sincerely hope so." He got out of the car, and Mann handed out his overnight bag. "I'll meet you in front of the Hofbräuhaus at eight o'clock sharp."

"Right," Mann said. "I'll have the rest of the things with me then."

Carter got a front room on the first floor. After he had shaved, showered, and changed into some clean clothes, he cleaned and oiled his weapons.

It was nearly noon before he went downstairs, had a light lunch and a beer in the restaurant, then rented a car and headed northwest past the magnificent Schloss Nymphenburg, once the summer residence of the kings of Bavaria.

A half mile beyond the palace's vast flower gardens and park, Carter cruised slowly by a Romanesque compound partially hidden behind tall stone walls.

This was the Soviet compound from which the trade delegation, on semipermanent assignment to Munich, operated. It was also where many of the Soviet consul's functions were maintained, and where many of the Aeroflot and Tass employees stayed. It had also long been known as an operations center for KGB activities in Germany, Austria, and Switzerland. To this point the Germans had tacitly accepted the compound's existence because it was easily watched. The Germans and the Americans felt that if they closed the place down, KGB operations outside of Berlin would go underground, and would be much more difficult to monitor.

The compound was surrounded on three sides by park and forestland. Only at the front was it open.

Carter parked his rental car a few blocks beyond the compound, and then as if he were simply a tourist out for an afternoon stroll in the park, he circled around to the back, to within fifty yards of the compound's walls.

From where he stood, Carter could just see the back of the main building within the compound. The roofline bristled with various antennae, all pointing east, back toward the geostationary satellite the Soviets used for communications relay with Moscow.

A West German Air Force helicopter suddenly clattered

into view just over the treetops. Carter stepped back against a tree so that he would be out of sight from the air, and watched as the chopper slowly made a pass over the Soviet compound, then disappeared in the distance.

From what Carter understood, these flyovers happened every two hours around the clock. He glanced at his watch. It was just two o'clock. It meant another flyover would be scheduled for four o'clock; then at six, eight, and ten, and throughout the night.

He turned away and went back to his car. At the ten o'clock flyover, the Soviets would be in for a surprise. A very large surprise.

Carter spent the remainder of the afternoon sightseeing, and generally making sure that if anyone wanted to tail him, it would be easy.

Shortly after seven he returned to his hotel, collected his things, and checked out. He told the desk clerk that a change of plans had necessitated his immediate departure for Garmisch-Partenkirchen, the resort town about fifty miles south of Munich, famous for its proximity to the Zugspitze, Germany's tallest mountain.

He had the clerk call ahead and make reservations in his name at the Alpina, a luxury hotel. Then he left a large tip and headed out of the city.

Six blocks from the hotel, he speeded up, and after twenty minutes of driving, sure that he had not picked up a tail, he doubled back, arriving in front of the Hofbräuhaus just at eight.

Mann was waiting for him. Carter pulled up beside the AXE resident's car, and wound down his window. Mann leaned over and cranked down his own window.

"Meet me at the compound, in the park just beyond," Carter said. "But make sure you're clean."

"Right," Mann said.

"Did you bring the things?"

Mann nodded. "Hawk called."

"I don't want to hear it," Carter said, rolling up his window. He crashed the gearshift into first and took off.

For the next half hour he concentrated on his driving, making absolutely certain he was not picking up a tail.

Mann was just pulling into the park area as Carter showed up.

It was very windy now, and cold, but the rain had eased to a misting drizzle, perfect for cover.

"No trouble?" Carter asked.

"None. You?"

"I'm clean," Carter said. He and Mann quickly changed into black jump suits, darkened their faces, and then pulled on the small packs Mann had brought along.

They headed immediately into the woods on a diagonal line that would bring them to the Soviet compound's back wall.

"What about security?" Carter asked as they walked.

"It's always been light. We don't bother them, except electronically, and they don't display any hardware."

"They must maintain a perimeter watch."

Mann nodded. "They usually have one or two men on the outside. But I couldn't tell you their schedule."

"Armed?"

"Probably."

They hurried the rest of the way in silence, eventually coming within sight of the ten-foot-high wall, where they crouched behind a tree to watch and listen for a few minutes.

Carter checked his watch. It was just past nine-thirty, which meant they had less than thirty minutes to get in, do their thing, and get back out before the West German Air Force chopper made its routine pass.

There were a couple of lights on in upstairs windows of the compound building. Other than that the place was mostly in darkness.

Carter and Mann made it the rest of the way to the wall, and

Mann boosted Carter up so that he could see over the top. Several cars were parked near what appeared to be a large service garage, and a light shone from around front. Other than that there was nothing to see.

Carter pulled himself the rest of the way up onto the wall, then, lying flat on his stomach, he reached down and helped Mann up and over the top.

Seconds later they both had dropped inside the compound and were racing to the back of the main building.

Mann pulled a grappling hook and line from his pack, and without hesitation he tossed it up, the hook catching on the edge of the roof three stories above.

"You've got everything you need in your pack," Mann whispered, looking around. "I've got the detonator radio. They're standard radio-controlled fuses, with plastique bricks."

"Stand by," Carter whispered. "If we have some company, shut them up, but don't kill anyone."

"Right," Mann said.

Carter quickly climbed up the rope, and at the top he rolled over onto the roof in the midst of the communications and surveillance antennae.

He looked back over the edge, but Mann had disappeared, probably on a scouting trip.

Working as fast as he could in the darkness, Carter attached plastique charges to all seven of the compound's antennae, inserting a radio-controlled fuse into each of the charges.

With eight minutes to spare he was again at the edge of the roof. Still Mann was not back. Carter eased over the eaves and quickly scrambled down the rope. With a quick flip on the line he had the grappling hook retrieved. He coiled the line and stuffed it into his pack as he headed around the corner on the run.

Charlie Mann was crouched in the shadows beside the

building. He urgently motioned for Carter to get down.

"Two guards out front. They've got the fence line to the side covered," Mann whispered.

Carter spotted the two Russians leaning against the side of a truck near the front of the building. They were talking.

Time was getting short. They were going to have to be out of there before the chopper came for its flyover.

Carter and Mann eased back around the corner, then stood up and headed in a dead run straight back away from the compound building, then around the corner of the service garage where they clambered over the wall.

With less than three minutes to go, Mann pulled the detonator out of his pack and set it for discharge as they hurried through the woods back toward their cars.

They had just come to the edge of the woods when the sound of the chopper's rotors came to them over the breeze.

Mann stopped and looked back as Carter peeled off his dark jump suit.

"Hold it," Carter said. "Hold it!"

The chopper came directly overhead, and a couple of seconds later it was directly over the Soviet compound.

"Now!" Carter snapped.

Mann cranked the switch, and an instant later a large explosion lit up the night sky.

"That'll give the bastards something to think about," Carter muttered.

"And the West Germans aren't going to be exactly over-joyed either," Mann said.

He and Carter raced back to their cars, tossing the packs and other things into the trunk of Mann's BMW.

"Good luck, Nick. It's been an interesting evening," Mann said.

They shook hands. "I'll clear you with Hawk when the dust settles," Carter said.

"Was it worth the trouble it's going to cause?"

"It was worth ten times as much trouble, my friend."

"Good enough for me," Mann said. "Take care, pal."

"Right," Carter said, and he jumped into his car and headed toward the E6 that led down to Garmisch-Partenkirchen, not turning on his headlights until he was well away from the now furiously burning Soviet compound.

Kobelev would put two and two together, and understand that the business tonight had been Carter's work. He would also find out within hours—if he didn't already know—that Carter would be at the Alpina Hotel.

Carter grinned. But that was just the beginning. He was going to play Kobelev's game back at the man in spades. Before this weekend was over, Sigourney's death would be avenged. When it came time for Carter to speak to her parents, he would have something positive to say to them.

THIRTEEN

It took an hour and a half to circle around Munich, then to drive south to Garmisch-Partenkirchen. During the trip down, Carter listened on the car radio to the first news reports of the explosion at the Soviet compound. A Soviet spokesman from Berlin said it was his understanding that the act may have been one of aggression by certain members of the West German Air Force.

The reaction had come a lot sooner and was much harsher than Carter had expected. Once the dust had settled, and it was discovered that the explosion had come not from the West Germans but had been an act of sabotage by unknown parties, it would not set well on Kobelev's record. It wouldn't take the KGB long to understand just who had engineered the raid. And then they would naturally turn to Comrade General Kobelev for an explanation: "Why wasn't Carter stopped sooner? Why wasn't he eliminated in the Caribbean when you had the opportunity and the means?" Carter could almost hear the outrage from Moscow, and he smiled.

Jealousy. Fear. Vengeance. Carter wondered which litany Kobelev would be willing to recite.

But then, he thought, all of that speculation was moot. By then Kobelev and his handmaiden Ganin would be dead if Carter had his way.

In the resort town, quiet now because it was between the summer season and the winter skiing season, Carter parked his car a block from the big hotel and with bag in hand went the rest of the way on foot.

He was checked in by an obsequious clerk. "Welcome to the Alpina, Herr Carter," the man gushed. "If there is anything at all we can do to make your stay more pleasant . . ."

"Are there any messages for me?" Carter asked irritably.

"No, sir."

"I wish to be awakened with breakfast at six o'clock sharp. Afterward I will be going to the Zugspitze. I wish to see it first thing in the morning."

"But, Herr Carter, the weather forecast for tomorrow is for continued rain and perhaps snow. You will not be able to see much . . ."

Carter just glared at the little man, who backed down.

"*Ja, mein Herr*. Six o'clock."

Upstairs in his room, Carter positioned himself on a straight-backed chair between the large double windows and the door, his Luger in hand, the safety off, a round in the firing chamber. It would be simpler if Ganin were to come through the door then and there.

But his message downstairs was clear. In the morning Carter would be atop the tallest mountain in Germany. There would be very few people there at that hour of the morning. It would be a perfect place. Carter's killing ground.

It was exactly six in the morning when room service arrived with a Continental breakfast of coffee, rolls, butter, and preserves, and the morning newspapers from Munich as well as a local paper from Garmisch-Partenkirchen.

Carter tipped the man, then settled down to his coffee.

The papers made only small mention of the Soviet compound explosion, which was not really surprising to Carter. The German government would be trying to suppress the story as much as possible. It was only natural considering the always strained relationship between the two countries.

On the back pages, however, there was the report of still two more deaths in avalanches near Innsbruck. Kobelev would continue killing people there until Carter came to him. It didn't matter to the madman how many innocent people were killed in the process. But he was going to get to Carter.

After breakfast, Carter took a shower, got dressed, and left the hotel. The overcast had deepened, and the temperature had plunged overnight. It was probably snowing in the mountains, Carter figured, a harsh contrast to the Caribbean of the previous week.

All through the night Carter's thoughts had alternated between Lydia and Sigourney. One was beyond his help, and it was possible the other was already dead as well.

In both instances he felt responsible. He felt that by making the mistake of allowing himself to get that one crucial step behind Kobelev, he had caused the end of at least one innocent life.

Mindful now that a bullet could be coming at any moment from any direction, Carter made his way from the hotel to where he had parked his rental car. Only a few early risers were up and about.

He got the engine started and let the car warm up for a couple of minutes before he eased out of the parking lot and slowly headed out of town, southwest toward the Zugspitze.

The highway wound its way up into the cloud-shrouded mountains toward the Austrian border just a mile away. The Zugspitze was right on the border. The enclosed cable car that ran to the restaurant and observation platform atop the mountain was at the end of a broad access road.

At the height of the summer season, this was normally a very busy spot. Germans as well as foreigners flocked here by the thousands on clear days when the views from the top were spectacular.

Carter turned off the highway and drove slowly down the access road to the parking lot beside the tourist shop and cable car boarding building.

A battered Volkswagen van was parked behind the tourist shop, and just beyond it a VW beetle was pulled up beneath the broad overhang of the roof.

Those belonged to the staff, Carter assumed. The only other vehicle in the large parking lot was a sleek, gunmetal gray Porsche 911, with Austrian plates. Probably a rental car.

Slowly he circled the Porsche, making reasonably sure that no one was inside before he parked beside it, his car pointed out toward the exit.

Leaving the keys in the ignition, he withdrew Wilhelmina, got out of his car, and slowly approached the Porsche. He stopped a couple of feet away, and glanced up toward the mountain. The cables rose at a sharp angle and disappeared into the mist within a hundred feet or so.

No one was in the Porsche. Inside, on the steering column, the registration slip showed that the car was from Innsbruck and belonged to Inter-Rent, an Austrian car rental agency.

Again Carter glanced up toward the mist-shrouded peak. The car was driven here by Arkadi Ganin. He knew it. He could feel the man's presence very strongly.

He holstered his Luger and withdrew his stiletto. Working very fast, he punctured all four tires on the sportscar, the Porsche settling to the pavement.

Back in his own car, he started it and slowly drove over to the tourist shop, where he parked it behind the van so that it was just barely visible from the parking lot.

He walked around to the front of the building, went up the steep concrete stairs below the cable car exit, and went inside. The room was very tall and narrow. Access to the cable car platform was through a tall canvas and plastic curtain. A huge section of that side of the building was open, the gigantic motors and cable pullies at the rear.

On the opposite side of the main room was a tourist counter and the ticket desk.

An old woman sat at the desk. She was writing something in a ledger. Beside her, piled on the counter, were various slips and receipts.

She looked up. "*Guten Morgen*," she said, her Bavarian accent thick.

"*Guten Morgen, gnädige Frau*," Carter said. "Is the cable car operating this morning?"

"Yes, of course. If I am here, then the car is working. You wish to go up . . . with the other strange one?"

"Someone else has gone up this morning?"

The old woman nodded. "A strange man."

"In what way was he strange?"

She shrugged. "Oh, I don't know. But let me tell you, I think he is a Russian, even though his German was very good."

Carter smiled. "And me?"

"You're an American, of course . . ." she started, and then she cut herself off and looked up toward the mountain. "Oh," she said.

Carter handed her money for the ride, and the old woman took it and handed him his ticket. "The restaurant will not open today. Not until Monday."

"*Danke*," Carter said. He went across to the heavy plastic curtain, pushed aside the flap, and climbed aboard the bright red cable car. The cabin was quite big and could probably hold a dozen or more people.

As soon as he had the door closed and latched, the car jerked on its cables and lifted free of the boarding platform. Carter glanced back toward the counter. The old woman had gone back to her ledger book, and then he was outside the building, being lifted up into the clouds.

On a clear day the ride up to the top of the Zugspitze was breathtaking. That morning the visibility was zero. Within a hundred feet of the cable house, the car was enveloped in a thick cloud, making it impossible to see anything but the gray, swirling mist.

A thousand feet up it began to snow, lightly, but in large flakes. If this kept up, Carter suspected they would close the lift. Too much snow made operating the cable car dangerous.

It was very cold at this altitude. Carter could see his breath.

A large tower suddenly loomed up, and they passed beside it, the pullies bumping on the tower's tracks, then it was gone.

Carter lit a cigarette, then pulled out Wilhelmina and checked to make sure a round was in the firing chamber. He clicked the safety off as they passed another tower, and suddenly the mountain top came into view, a lone man standing on the broad veranda of the closed restaurant.

It was Ganin!

Carter looked for the latch that would open the cable car's window, noting Ganin's hand coming up. The Killmaster fell back into the corner of the car as the window glass was shattered. Two other shots whined off the side of the car before it slid into the upper terminal building.

For a few moments Ganin was out of sight. Carter leaped up on the inside handrails, flipped open the car's rooftop access hatch, and quickly pulled himself up, closing the hatch behind him.

He lay on his stomach as the car bumped to a halt. A second later Ganin came across the broad lobby from the veranda, and Carter snapped off two shots just as the car jerked beneath him. Both shots went wide and Ganin spun to the left, diving out of sight around the corner.

Carter rolled off the edge of the car, jumped down to the

concrete platform, and leaped behind a steel support column, a single shot ricocheting off the steel inches from his head.

It was quiet in the building. Carter could hear the rising wind beginning to hum through the cables outside.

"You're not going to leave this mountain alive, Nick Carter!" Ganin called from around the corner.

"In that case you won't mind telling me where Lydia Borasova is being kept," Carter shouted.

Ganin laughed. "Are you in love . . . again, Carter? Haven't you learned your lesson?"

Carter said nothing.

"She is with Kobelev, in Innsbruck," Ganin said.

"Where in Innsbruck?"

"It does not matter, Carter."

"It matters to me, because after I kill you, I'm going to kill Kobelev," Carter said. He peered around the edge of the steel beam. There was a door at the rear of the cable car terminal that probably led back into the restaurant, or perhaps a storeroom.

There was silence in the lobby.

"Ganin?" Carter shouted. "It cannot hurt to tell me."

"They are staying in a chalet."

"Where?" Carter asked. He edged around the beam.

"At Axamer Lizum."

"Where the winter Olympics were held?"

"Yes, that is the place," Ganin said.

"Who else is with them?" Carter shouted, almost smiling; Ganin was so sure he would get Carter, he didn't think twice about giving him the information. He stepped around the beam and, keeping on the balls of his feet, raced to the rear door. It was unlocked.

"They are alone . . ." Ganin was saying as Carter slipped into a storeroom for the kitchen.

He raced down a narrow aisle, then through a set of swinging doors into the kitchen itself. From there he went out into the dining room, then hurried around to the front, and to the lobby.

Ganin was not there.

It took just a split second for Carter to realize that the Russian had probably come right behind him. He spun around the corner, bringing his Luger up, as Ganin came from the kitchen, the Russian's gun aimed at Carter's chest.

Carter fired first, catching Ganin in the shoulder, shoving him backward into the kitchen.

Ganin fired twice as he fell, a hot stitch lacing into Carter's side, causing him to drop back.

The shot had been impossible, yet Ganin had missed killing Carter by less than two inches.

Carter watched the kitchen doors swing on their hinges for several moments before he slipped around the corner, and keeping low, he zigzagged to the wall beside the doorway.

There were no sounds from within the kitchen. Carter eased around the edge and looked through the window. The kitchen was empty. A trail of blood led across the white tile floor to a door on the opposite side of the room.

That was the sucker's route. Ganin most likely would be waiting just beyond the far door, covering the entire kitchen, waiting for Carter to barge through.

Carter turned on his heel, and more cautiously now than before, he hurried back to the lobby, which wrapped around the front and two sides of the restaurant complex perched on the peak. Outside was the veranda, which afforded a magnificent view on clear days. Now it was snowing in earnest, and the wind was beginning to rise.

Hugging the inner wall, Carter hurried around to the left. Just around the corner he pulled up short. A tall husky man lay on his side, his eyes open. He was dead. A small puddle of blood had formed on the floor just below the back of his head.

Carter guessed the dead man had been in charge of that end

of the cable car run. Ganin had killed him.

A gust of cold wind suddenly blasted down the lobby and then was cut off.

Ganin was outside. Evidently he had made his way from the kitchen to the lobby, and then out onto the veranda.

Carter turned back and ran to the cable car terminal, where he opened the outside door and eased out onto the veranda.

A bullet whined off the concrete, and Carter snapped off a shot at Ganin's fleeing figure as it darted around the far corner.

Keeping low, Carter raced to the corner, then flattened against the wall before he peered around the edge.

The veranda was empty. Carter stepped around and walked to the far side, which ended abruptly at a stone wall, the drop further protected by a tall wire mesh fence.

Carter spotted the ladder that led up to the roof of the restaurant at the same moment he heard the distinctive snap of a pistol's hammer dropping on either an empty chamber or a defective shell.

He looked up, bringing Wilhelmina around as Ganin disappeared over the peak of the roof. Carter scrambled up the ladder, and at the edge he cautiously looked up. Ganin was nowhere in sight, but a trail of blood went from the edge to the peak above.

"Ganin!" Carter shouted.

There was no reply, only the wind.

"Ganin, give up! I won't kill you if you give up."

Ganin appeared at the roof's peak twenty feet to the left, and he pulled the trigger of his gun, but nothing happened.

Carter held back from firing. Ganin's gun had jammed. He holstered Wilhelmina and withdrew his stiletto, then climbed up onto the roof, making his way to the peak.

Just over the edge he looked down in time to see Ganin on the far side of the building, very near the edge, below which was a sheer drop of more than a thousand feet.

"No!" Carter shouted.

Ganin looked back and grinned.

Carter suddenly realized that the Russian knew what he was doing. Evidently below the roof was another part of the veranda.

Ganin scrambled for the eaves, intending to swing over the edge and drop down.

Carter brought his knife arm back and threw his stiletto with every ounce of his strength. The blade caught Ganin high in the shoulder just as he was heaving himself over the edge.

He let out a short, sharp cry and then was gone.

Carter slid down to the edge of the roof and looked over. Below and to the right was a ten-foot-square platform, evidently used as an access for several electrical cables coming up the side of the mountain.

Straight down was a sheer cliff, the distance lost in the snow and mist.

There was some blood on the edge of the platform's rail, but not on the platform itself.

Ganin had tried to make the platform but had just missed. He was dead now. Far below on the rocks.

Carter eased back away from the edge and clambered up over the peak and down the other side, where he descended the ladder back to the veranda.

Inside, he found a back corridor and maintenance area that led to a door that opened onto the platform.

He stepped out onto it and leaned over the edge to look down. There was nothing. Only the blood on the rail.

It was truly over. Ganin was dead. Now it was time for Innsbruck and Kobelev.

Carter turned, went back inside, and then followed the lobby back around to the cable car terminal. Aboard the car he picked up the telephone and called down to the woman in the terminal.

"Hello?" she shouted.

"The maintenance man for the car is busy. Would you please bring me down?" Carter said.

"What about the . . . other one?"

"He will be staying a while longer."

"Yes, all right," the woman said. And a moment later the car lurched and headed down.

Arkadi Ganin waited a full ten minutes after Carter had left, and then he painfully climbed back up the metal support struts that held the platform in place.

Two of his fingers were broken from the fall, and he was bleeding quite a bit from the stiletto wound.

It had been a very close call for him this time, all because of a jammed pistol and his own pride. Once again he had underestimated Carter. Only now he was at the advantage. Carter was convinced he was dead. The American would not think to look over his shoulder.

Ganin carefully climbed up the iron strut, then reached out for the edge of the platform. Slowly he managed to haul himself up beneath the rail, where he rolled over and lay on his back for a long time.

After the pain began to subside in his hand and in his shoulder, Ganin got shakily to his feet and tried the door. It was locked.

He looked up. Without hesitation he climbed carefully up on the rail, reached up, and caught the eaves of the roof with his fingers.

Pushing off with his feet, he managed to get a better grip, and with iron muscles and a will to match, he pulled himself up onto the roof.

A couple of minutes later he was climbing down the ladder to the veranda.

Inside, he located the restaurant's office, where he searched for and found a first aid kit. He bandaged up his fingers, binding them around a pencil, and then awkwardly cleaned and bandaged his shoulder wound.

In the kitchen he jimmied open one of the refrigerators, where he found makings for a sandwich.

In another refrigerator he found the beer. Bringing his food and drink out to the main dining room, he sat down, put his feet up and took a deep drink.

He would give Carter a full hour to get away before he called for the cable car. He would have to take care of the woman below and then telephone Kobelev to tell him what had happened. The drive down to Innsbruck would take only an hour.

He could see Carter in his sights. He could almost feel the satisfaction it would give him to see the back of Carter's head being blown off.

This time there would be no mistakes. This time pride would not get in the way. No matter what, Carter was a dead man.

FOURTEEN

Carter drove back into Garmisch-Partenkirchen and bought some bandages, gauze, and an antiseptic cream, then he went to his hotel. He cleaned up and afterward bandaged the wound in his side. It was superficial but painful.

In his mind's eye he kept seeing Ganin going over the edge. He kept seeing the blood on the platform rail. It bothered him that he hadn't actually seen the Russian's body. But surviving such a fall was a total impossibility. Yet something nagged at the back of Carter's brain. Some little thing he was overlooking. But he was too tired now to pursue it.

When he was ready he went downstairs to check out and pay his bill.

"Ah, Herr Carter," the desk manager said. "You received a telephone message just a minute ago." The man handed across a slip of paper.

Carter opened it and read the message. It was from Kobelev in Innsbruck: *We're waiting for your arrival . . . Lydia and I. Only wish dear Sigourney could have been here as well.*

161

Kobelev couldn't know that Ganin was dead. Not this soon. Yet he had to know that Ganin had come to the Zugspitze gunning for Carter.

The message had to be nothing more than Kobelev covering all the angles. On the chance that Carter either killed Ganin or somehow escaped, this message would be one more incentive to lure him to Innsbruck.

"Is something wrong, Herr Carter?" the manager was asking.

Carter looked up. "On the contrary," he said, forcing a smile. "Did the caller leave a return number?"

"*Nein, mein Herr*. I'm afraid not."

"It doesn't matter. But if he should happen to call back, tell him I'm on my way."

"Of course, sir," the clerk said.

"*Danke*," Carter said, and he left the hotel, climbed into his car, and headed southeast this time, back up into the mountains toward the Austrian border at Scharnitz, barely fifteen miles away.

Sooner or later the carnage at the top of the Zugspitze would be discovered. It was important that he be out of the country before then. He was reasonably sure the woman clerk would remember him, and it wouldn't take the police very long to track him back to the hotel.

Once he got to Innsbruck he was going to have to ditch the car. Keeping it would make it too easy for the Austrian police to catch up with him.

Carter was tired, and it seemed as if every bone in his body ached. He had begun the assignment without fully recuperating from the last. And he had collected his share of bumps and bruises during the past few days.

Ganin was dead. That thought kept running over and over again in his mind. Surely Kobelev would not be alone in Innsbruck. He would have his lieutenants. His goons would be around him, and they would be especially alert once it was learned Ganin had been killed.

If Kobelev were dug in at his chalet, he would be impossible to approach without placing Lydia in extreme danger.

As Carter drove, a plan began to formulate in his mind. Fight fire with fire; play Kobelev at his own game with audacity and arrogance. In the open where anyone who cared to could watch.

Kobelev would be lured out of his rat's nest just as he had lured Carter all across Europe.

At the border Carter's papers were checked, and he had to purchase additional liability insurance in order to drive in Austria. On the other side he exchanged the last of his German marks and some American dollars for Austrian shillings, then continued through Seefeld and Zirl in a heavy snowstorm, arriving in the lovely town of Innsbruck by early afternoon.

To the north was the Nordkette range of the Alps, and to the south, the Tuxer range; the city nestled between them. Carter had been here before some years ago, and he remembered that on a clear day the view from Innsbruck's main street, the Maria-Theresienstrasse, was magnificent.

Because of the early snowfall there was an air of excitement in the city. Soon the winter ski season would be in full swing, and the city would bustle with activity.

Parking his car downtown, Carter went to a couple of ski equipment and clothing shops, and outfitted himself with some very good equipment and expensive clothing.

Then he drove to the railroad station and checked his overnight bag and new purchases in several lockers. Finally, he drove the car back across town, where he parked it in a back lot at the university.

Carter caught a bus back to the station, where he retrieved his bags, then he stepped outside as if he had just arrived by train.

A taxi pulled up and Carter got in, ordering the driver to take him out to the Schlosshotel in Igls, which along with Axamer Lizum—where Kobelev was apparently staying in a private chalet—was a part of the Innsbruck winter sports area.

The hotel was a luxury spa for very wealthy people who wanted to come for the hot baths, various mineral and salt cures, and of course for the skiing and the Innsbruck night life.

Carter checked in with a lot of fanfare, opening an account with an unlimited ceiling on his platinum Carte Blanche.

"Are any of the slopes open yet?" he asked the clerk in the palatial lobby.

"Yes, sir, here, and of course at Axamer, the upper slopes have been opened," the clerk said, eying Carter. "But may I suggest, sir, that you first avail yourself of our hot mineral pool, and perhaps a series of muscle toners."

"Indeed," Carter sniffed. "Why did you think I came here in the first place?"

"Of course, sir."

The bellman helped Carter up to his beautiful rooms on the third floor, the view from which on a nice day was probably magnificent.

Carter tipped the man extremely well, then ordered up a bottle of champagne and a quarter pound of beluga caviar with toast points, grated onion, egg, and lemon.

Next he called the desk and arranged for a tailor to be sent up immediately.

While he was waiting he put Pierre in a drawer in the night stand beside the bed, and Wilhelmina under the pillow. He missed his stiletto.

His food and wine came within ten minutes, followed immediately by the tailor, who efficiently took his measurements.

"I'll need a tuxedo—plain, black, single-breasted—in time for this evening's dinner. And I need a blazer, a tweed sportcoat or two, and perhaps a couple of business suits. I'll leave fabrics to your discretion," Carter said.

Unfazed, the tailor was writing it all down.

"Of course I'll need shirts, ties, shoes, accessories."

"Very good, sir. Your luggage, perhaps, was lost?"

"By the stupid Germans."

The tailor raised his eyebrows knowingly. "It shall be as you wish, sir."

When the tailor was gone, Carter poured himself a glass of champagne and helped himself to the caviar. Very quickly the word would spread: an American is at the Schlosshotel. Very rich. Eccentric. Name is Nick Carter.

Kobelev would hear, and sooner or later he would have to come out himself to see.

Later in the afternoon, Carter spent a half hour scouting around the hotel, looking for bolt-holes for himself in case Kobelev made a frontal attack and tried to corner him.

Aside from the easy climb down from his balcony, he discovered several alternate means of escape. The hotel was very large. Stairways, corridors, and elevators seemed to be placed at random.

Back in his room he called for a masseur, who arrived within minutes pushing a long, padded table that he set up by the window.

He was a large man, Spanish, and very powerful. He did not speak a word as he arranged Carter on the table and began.

His touch was gentle and very professional, and soon Carter began to feel like a human being again.

The man was careful when he came to Carter's various wounds and bruises, and a half hour later when he was finished, and Carter sat up, he nodded.

"You have certainly been around, Señor Carter," he said. "Your right knee needs some help. Perhaps I will return tomorrow."

"Perhaps," Carter said noncommittally.

A half hour after the masseur left, the tailor returned with his tuxedo, shoes, a couple of formal shirts, and the other accessories.

"Your other things will be ready first thing in the morning, Herr Carter," the man said.

Carter tried on the suit. It fit perfectly. "My compliments," he said.

"One must look one's best for dinner here," the little man said, then he turned on his heel and left.

At seven Carter dressed for dinner, strapping on his Luger and positioning the little gas bomb. Downstairs, before he went into the bar, he made reservations at the front desk, for skiing on the upper slopes at Axamer for first thing in the morning. The hotel car and driver would be ready out front at eight o'clock sharp.

Then he went inside, ordered a scotch, and sat at the end of the bar, from where he had a clear view of the entrance to the lobby.

By now Kobelev would have to know about Ganin, and he would certainly be aware of Carter's presence in Innsbruck. The next move would be the Russian's, either that evening, or certainly the next morning sometime on the slopes.

Carter had given the man a choice: there at the hotel, or out on the slopes of the mountain somewhere. It would be dangerous. But Carter wanted the man drawn out.

The barman had moved to the opposite end of the bar, and he was talking on the telephone. He looked down toward Carter, then unplugged the telephone and brought it to him. He plugged it in behind the bar.

"A telephone call for you, Herr Carter," he said, holding out the instrument.

Carter looked at him for a moment, then nodded and took the phone. The opening shots already?

"Carter here," he said.

"Ah, Nicholas," Kobelev said. "You are enjoying your stay? I understand the Schlosshotel is lovely."

"I've come for you," Carter said softly.

"Yes, I know. And I'm delighted that you arrived safe and sound, though I do feel sorry for poor Arkadi. Unfortunate, that."

Carter said nothing.

"You did create quite a stir in Germany, you know. First in Munich, and then at the Zugspitze. And I tried to capitalize on it, you know, but to no avail. Your David Hawk is quite good."

"Tell me, are you returning to Moscow so that you can kill little children in safety?" Carter taunted. "I mean, now that you no longer have Ganin to run your errands?"

Kobelev laughed. "On the contrary, Nicholas. Tomorrow I expect to see you at the slopes over here. I'm quite looking forward to it, you know. I still have not forgotten my daughter, or the Orient Express. It's taken me two years to recover. And I am a man who never forgets."

Carter had made reservations for skiing less than ten minutes earlier. It meant that Kobelev had people at the hotel who were watching him. Probably someone at the front desk.

"What do you want, then? Why wait until tomorrow?"

"The impatience of youth," Kobelev sighed. "I wish you to be fit. To be well rested for our encounter in the morning."

Carter looked up at that moment in time to see Lydia Borasova coming through the doorway from the lobby. She wore a low-cut sequined evening dress and a short sable jacket thrown casually over her shoulders. Her blond hair was done up. She looked lovely.

"I've sent along a little present for you. To the victor goes the spoils, I believe you once said."

Lydia spotted Carter at the bar and came across to him. She was trying her best to smile for the benefit of the other people at the bar, but Carter could see she was barely holding on.

"Enjoy her for tonight, Nicholas. Believe me, enjoy the whore, because by noon tomorrow both of you will be dead." Kobelev hung up.

"It was him?" Lydia asked, sitting down next to Carter.

Carter hung up the phone. The bartender came to collect it, and he placed a cocktail napkin in front of Lydia.

"Madam?"

"Vodka," she said. "No ice." She turned back to Carter, her eyes glistening. "He is crazy with rage. He killed my father, and he promises to kill my mother unless I do as he says."

Carter touched her hand. "I'm sorry . . ."

"They came to the hotel. There wasn't a thing I could do. God, I am so frightened, Nick. He has others in Germany. When they told him you had killed Ganin he went berserk. It was terrible. I thought he was going to kill me then and there."

"What happened?" Carter asked. "Why did he let you go?"

"It's no use, you know," she said. Her drink came. She tossed it back and pushed her glass forward for another. The bartender complied, then moved off to the far end of the bar.

"He has people here at the hotel?"

She nodded. "This town is his," she said. "He has at least a hundred men and women in his entourage. You can't go anywhere or do anything without them knowing about it."

"What about the Austrian police?"

"He's got them as well, somehow. They won't touch him unless he becomes so obvious as to involve a private citizen. They are happy to let this be solely between you and him. And he will kill you; there is no doubt in my mind. He has the people."

"But he'll want to be present. He'll want to see it happen."

"Yes. He wants to pull the trigger himself. All he can talk about is you."

Was it too much? Carter wondered. Kobelev never did a thing without a very good reason. Had he sent Lydia to lull him into a false sense of security for the night?

Kobelev could talk about no one else other than Carter? Was it so? Once again, Carter got the feeling that he was missing something. Missing some piece of information crucial to his own survival. But what?

Lydia was studying his face as he thought.

"Is it true?" she asked. "Is Ganin dead?"

Carter started to answer yes, but then he held off. Was Ganin dead? He saw the man go over the edge. He saw the blood on the rail.

Suddenly another thought crossed his mind, and he went cold. Suddenly he realized just what it was that had bothered him. Ganin. *Christ, is it possible?*

In his mind's eye he went back to the Zugspitze. He put himself in Ganin's spot. Ganin turned around at the edge of the roof and smiled. He smiled! He had a means of escape worked out.

In his mind, Carter let himself fall over the edge. The balcony railing came up at him, and he grabbed it. An instant later, a split second later he swung himself under the balcony to a platform, or perhaps to a beam on the supporting structure. Beneath the balcony!

After Carter had left, Ganin had climbed up, taken the cable car down, and stolen one of the staff cars parked behind the cable car building.

Ganin. Alive. It was just possible.

"What is it?" Lydia asked, alarmed. She had read something of that in his eyes.

"Ganin is alive," Carter said softly. "Or at least there is a very good possibility he is alive."

Lydia's hand went to her mouth. "I thought—"

"Kobelev is convinced I believe Ganin is dead. Tomorrow he says the confrontation will come. He sent you along, and that was his mistake."

"I don't understand."

"Tonight I supposedly will be lulled into a sense of false security. You and I will be so happy to see each other that I will be off my guard. He did the same thing last time with . . . Sigourney."

"Ganin will come here? Tonight?"

"I'm sure of it."

Lydia looked away, pale. "I'll never escape. It is impossible."

"No," Carter said. "Ganin and Kobelev will never leave Innsbruck alive. They've made a fatal mistake."

She looked into his eyes, wanting to believe him, but she finally looked away.

They had a lovely dinner in the hotel's excellent restaurant, and Carter made a great show of fawning all over Lydia as if he were a starved lover and could hardly wait to get her upstairs in bed. He also seemed to be drinking a great deal of wine.

Afterward he tipped too heavily, and he and Lydia made sure they were spotted crossing the lobby and taking the elevator up to his room.

The information would get back to Kobelev. Immediately. Ganin, in turn, would be set loose. But Carter was sure that if Ganin were alive, and in any kind of shape to come there, he would have to be a changed, much more cautious man. That, too, would be the assassin's undoing.

Two suitcases were stacked in the middle of the bedroom floor.

"They're mine," Lydia said. "I had them sent up."

"Could there be explosives . . ."

She shook her head. "I thought the same thing. I packed them myself."

For the next twenty minutes, Carter methodically checked the room from top to bottom, making sure there were no listening devices, no bombs or hidden booby traps of any kind, and then he double-locked the main door, shoving the heavy living room couch in front of it. In the bedroom he made sure the windows were locked and the drapes pulled closed. With great effort he managed to move the massive wardrobe, built of solid oak, in front of the windows. It wouldn't stop a determined assassin, of course, but it would slow him down and deny him a noiseless entrance.

Lydia watched him work with wide eyes. "Do you think this will stop him?"

"No, just slow him down," Carter said. "Buy us some time." He peeled off his clothes and took a quick shower.

When he came out, Lydia was sitting cross-legged on the floor smoking one of his cigarettes and drinking a glass of champagne. She had tossed her jacket aside, and her dress was hiked up to her hips.

"They could have poisoned the wine," Carter said, coming across to her.

"Not his style," she said.

Carter sat down beside her, and she poured him some champagne, and held the cigarette to his lips so that he could take a puff.

"A celebration," she said. "One way or another I will be free within twenty-four hours." She laughed. "Either he kills us, or you kill them. And then my worries will be over."

It was the fatalistic Russian attitude. It was common.

She leaned over and kissed Carter, lightly at first, but then she placed the cigarette into the rest of her champagne, set the glass aside, then got up on her knees and pulled off her dress.

She wore no bra, and her nipples were erect. She slid out of her panties, and pressed Carter back on the carpet, pulling off the towel he had wrapped around his waist.

"Live or die," she said seriously. "It does not matter. I want you to make love to me now, Nick Carter. For the last time, no matter what happens."

They kissed deeply, and then she worked her way down his

chest, across his stomach, finally taking him in her mouth.

Carter reached down and undid her hair, pleasure coursing through his body, as she did magical things with her tongue, lips, and fingers, trying to lose herself in lovemaking.

She sat up suddenly, tears streaming from her eyes. "I need you," she said in Russian. "Please?"

Carter rolled her gently over onto her back, and she opened her legs, pulling him to her, and they made love, slowly at first, but then faster and harder with more urgency, until Lydia cried out in passion and fear at the very end.

FIFTEEN

The dawn broke very cold and gray. Carter got up from where he had been sitting in the middle of the living room all night and splashed some cold water on his face.

Lydia had crawled off to bed, but she had not gone to sleep until sometime after four in the morning. It was barely seven now, and she was wide awake.

"He didn't come," she said when Carter emerged from the bathroom.

"No," Carter said. He went into the living room and pulled the couch aside. Then he went to the phone and ordered eggs and sausage and toast, with plenty of coffee for both of them.

Ganin hadn't come. Which meant he *was* dead after all, or he had learned his lesson and was waiting until Carter left the security of the hotel.

Back in the bathroom, Carter took a quick shower, then shaved and got dressed in his new ski clothes. Their breakfast came a few minutes later, and after the room service waiter had left, Carter sat down with a cup of coffee and slowly cleaned Wilhelmina.

Lydia watched it all, and then joined him for their breakfast, although neither of them ate very much.

Afterward she got dressed, and they repacked their bags and Carter's ski equipment.

"What happens now?" she asked. "I cannot remain here like this."

"No," Carter said. "You're going to Munich. Then back to the States."

"I won't be able to cross the frontier. I have no passport."

"You'll be met," Carter said. "At Scharnitz. Do you know where it is?"

She nodded. "On the way back to Garmisch-Partenkirchen," she said. "But how?"

"You'll see," Carter said.

They left their room and went downstairs to the lobby, Carter's right hand in his jacket pocket, his fingers curled around the grip of his Luger.

The desk clerk said nothing as Carter signed his charge slip and checked out.

"Is the car ready to take me skiing?" Carter asked.

"Of course, sir, but I thought . . ." the clerk said, flustered. After hearing reports of the American's overindulgence the night before, he was amazed to see him standing this early, let alone ready to ski.

Carter grinned. "I'm meeting an old friend on the slopes. I wouldn't miss it for the world."

"Yes, sir," the clerk said. "I'll have the car brought around immediately."

Carter figured the clerk was very likely in Kobelev's employ.

The Killmaster and Lydia crossed the lobby, and a couple of minutes later the hotel car, a Mercedes 300D, pulled up outside. The driver, a tall, very husky young man with blond hair, jumped out and helped them with their bags.

They headed away from the hotel, and when they were

down on the main highway that led over to Axamer, Carter ordered the driver to turn around and make a stop in Innsbruck first.

"Sir?" the driver asked, glancing up into the rearview mirror and not slowing down.

"Innsbruck," Carter said. He pulled out Wilhelmina and laid the end of the barrel against the base of the driver's skull. He too probably worked for Kobelev.

"Yes, sir," the man said. A hundred yards down the road he pulled around, and they hurried back into town.

He directed the driver to pull up in front of the train station, and then he handed his Luger to Lydia. "Hold him for a couple of minutes. I'll get your tickets."

"Don't leave me," Lydia protested.

"I'll just be a minute," Carter said, and he jumped out of the car, went inside, and angled directly over to the telephones.

He placed a call to Charlie Mann in Munich. "Do you know who this is?"

"Jesus H. Christ, you're the last person I figured I'd hear from today. All hell is breaking loose down here."

"How fast can you get to Scharnitz with a passport for a woman named Lydia Borasova? Blond. Pretty. Russian."

There was silence on the line for a moment or two.

"Three hours tops. She hot?"

"Very. I want her back in D.C. as soon as possible. Call Smitty. He'll know what to do with her."

"What about you?"

"Don't ask. Just get to Scharnitz as fast as possible. She'll be waiting on the Austrian side in the beer garden."

"Will do," Mann said, and Carter hung up.

Back outside, he climbed into the car, took the Luger from Lydia, and ordered the driver to take them over to the university.

Keeping his hands out of sight of the driver, Carter carefully passed the rental car's keys to Lydia, making sure she could see the tag that described the car and gave its license plate number. He mouthed the single word *Scharnitz*. She nodded.

They got to the university, and the driver pulled over to the curb. Carter embraced Lydia and whispered, "Car's in the back lot. A friend named Charlie Mann will be waiting for you at the beer garden. Good luck."

When they parted, Carter glanced at the driver, then back to Lydia. "Your train leaves in a couple of hours. You can stay here at the university, in the library, until then. You'll be safe."

She nodded again. "Have a good day skiing."

"Sure," Carter said.

Lydia got out of the car and hurried into the university. The driver watched her go, his eyes narrowed.

"Now it's time for the slopes," Carter said. "Axamer."

The driver glanced at Carter's reflection in the mirror, then pulled away from the curb, back the way they had come.

Twenty minutes later they had turned off the highway and followed the road back up to Axamer, higher up in the mountains.

Around a large curve, they came to the sports complex where in 1964 and again in 1976 the winter Olympics had been held.

There were quite a few cars in the vast parking lot despite the fact that the ski season hadn't really begun yet. But the recent heavy snowfalls had helped speed things up.

Carter pocketed his Luger as they pulled up to the main building, and the driver turned around to him.

"Listen to me, for what it's worth," Carter said. "I'm getting out here. I want you to turn around and drive directly back to the hotel. If I see you again, for whatever reason, I will kill you immediately. No questions, no arguments, I will kill you. Do you understand?"

The young man swallowed hard, his earlier confidence gone under the direct threat. "Yes, sir."

"Fine," Carter said, and he climbed out of the car, got his things from the trunk, then without looking back went into the main building. He bought an all-day, all-slopes lift ticket and went outside.

After standing his skis and poles in one of the racks, he put on his ski boots, then walked up onto the balcony where he took a table near the railing and ordered himself a coffee and schnapps.

The overcast had lifted somewhat, although it looked as if it might snow again at any moment. Rising above were the magnificent slopes of the Austrian Alps. From where he sat he could see quite a few skiers descending in zigzag patterns, the lifts rising up into the sky, and off to the west the village with its private, very expensive chalets.

This then, at last, was the killing ground. Today was the killing day. Somewhere very near were Kobelev and his goons. And very probably Ganin, too.

His coffee came, and he sipped it as he smoked a cigarette and watched the skiers rise up on the chair lifts and then descend the slopes.

Ski conditions were wonderful for this early, and there was a festive, holiday mood at the lodge.

Carter stiffened and sat forward. Seventy-five yards away, at the chair lift entry point, a tall, well-built man was getting aboard a chair. It was Ganin. Carter was sure of it.

The chair took off, and Ganin turned around and looked directly at Carter. He waved, and then the lift seemed to accelerate upward.

Carter threw down a twenty-shilling note, hurried off the balcony, quickly put on his skis, and skied over to the chair lift entry point.

He was only fourth in line, and within three minutes of sighting Ganin, he was on a chair going up into the mountains.

On the way up he lifted his skis and checked his bindings to make sure they were set for extremely stiff conditions, then he pulled out Wilhelmina to make sure she was ready to fire.

Ganin, he kept thinking. The man was absolutely incredible. Without a doubt one of the very best Carter had ever gone up against in his long career. Between Ganin's abilities and Kobelev's perverse genius, they were an awesome force.

The chair lift followed the slope up at an extreme angle. At times the chair was two hundred feet above the mountainside, while at other times it dropped to treetop level.

Within a few minutes the lodge was lost below in the mist. The chair rose up over the top of a tower, then started to dip down again, closer to the steeply sloping ground.

A bullet whined off the metal armrest beside Carter, and he lurched to the left.

A lone skier below and to the left had a rifle up to his shoulder. Carter violently swung the chair to the right as a second shot snapped by so close that Carter could feel the wind of its passage.

He yanked out his Luger and snapped off a single shot despite the impossible distance.

The gunman lowered the rifle and took off, skiing down the slopes.

Carter looked up a moment later in time to see a helicopter appear out of the mists from the west. The passenger door was open, and someone was hanging half out of the machine, a rifle in his hands.

The chair was fifty feet off the ground at this point. The helicopter was closing in fast.

Without hesitation Carter shoved himself off, ducking low as he fell. For the first moment or two he was in danger of losing his balance, and tumbling, but he managed to straighten out and twist his body around so that he was facing down the slope, and he leaned way out as if he had just launched himself from a tall ski jump scaffold.

He was being fired at from the helicopter as well as from the ground, which was racing up at him with incredible suddenness.

Carter braced himself for the tremendous shock of landing, and when he hit he nearly lost it. An instant later he had his balance and was schussing down the extremely steep slope in excess of seventy miles per hour, the moguls driving his bent knees nearly to his chest, his injured leg threatening to collapse beneath him at any moment.

Slowly, cautiously he began to have better control and began making a wide, arcing turn to the east toward a broad stand of pine, his speed slowing, a huge rooster tail of snow carved by the fantastic accelerations rising high.

The helicopter was directly above him as Carter came to a full stop, falling sideways, end over end, Wilhelmina still in hand.

He looked up at the machine, the howling gale from the rotors so close overhead making it all but impossible to see much of anything.

Carter caught a glimpse of Kobelev himself strapped on the passenger side, hanging half out of the doorway, an automatic rifle at his shoulder. Bullets were spraying everywhere around Carter, but he calmly raised his Luger and began firing slowly, one careful shot at a time into the blinding snow. The first went wide, but Carter was sure he hit Kobelev with the second. The third hit the engine and the fourth a rotor.

The machine suddenly lurched downslope and turned over on its side, Kobelev still hanging half out of the open doorway, and finally disappeared into a broad copse of trees. Seconds later a ball of flame rose from the trees, followed by the harsh crump of a big explosion.

Carter got to his feet, the sounds of distant avalanches set off by the explosion rumbling all around, and spotted a lone skier coming down the slopes from above.

It was Ganin!

Carter dropped back to one knee, brought Wilhelmina up, and took careful aim at the figure speeding toward him. His finger was on the trigger, Ganin was lined up perfectly in his sights, but a moment later Carter lowered his gun.

Not that way, he told himself.

He got up, took off his skis, and stepped aside, the Luger pointed down.

When Ganin got to within a dozen yards of where Carter stood waiting, he pulled up short in a burst of snow and stepped sideways. He pulled off his gloves and tossed them aside.

"Under the balcony?" Carter asked.

"It was very difficult. I nearly missed," Ganin said. He held up his left hand. Two of his fingers were bandaged. "Broken."

Carter nodded. The man was indeed incredible. "Kobelev is dead."

Ganin glanced beyond Carter, where a few hundred yards down the slope flames rose from the trees. He nodded. "This time you should check to make sure he is actually dead. See the body. Remember Bulgaria."

"First there is you," Carter said.

Ganin shook his head. "I have no quarrel with you, Carter. In fact I have a great deal of respect for you."

"I can't let you walk away from here."

"You will shoot me down in cold blood?"

"If need be. There is still the business of the poor Frenchman in Borodin's apartment building. And the caretaker at Zugspitze."

Ganin shrugged. "Casualties of war."

"No," Carter said.

"I see," Ganin replied. But then he leaped on his skis and suddenly flashed downslope. "Here!" he shouted.

Carter's own stiletto came out of nowhere, burying itself to the hilt in his gun arm. Carter fell back, shifting Wilhelmina to his left, and snapped off two shots, both of them hitting Ganin before he got another ten yards, and the Russian went down in a heap, tumbling end over end, for another thirty yards before he lay still.

For a long time Carter remained crouched where he was in the snow, his Luger wavering between the flames still rising from the trees and Ganin's body.

Was it over? At long last was it finished?

At length Carter painfully got to his feet, stepped into his skis, and unsteadily skied down to Ganin. He pocketed his Luger as he pulled up, and released his skis.

For a second Carter just stared at the Russian. Suddenly he realized Ganin's boots were out of his ski bindings.

He started to reach for his Luger, when Ganin reared up like some enraged animal, leaping onto Carter, both of them falling back into the snow.

Ganin was extraordinarily strong despite his injuries, despite two 9mm Luger bullets in his back; his fingers curled powerfully around Carter's neck, cutting off the air.

They rolled over, and as the world began to go dark, Carter gave one last mighty heave, getting his left arm free. He reached around, yanked the stiletto out of his right arm, and plunged it into Ganin's back.

The Russian bellowed and rose up as Carter yanked out the razor-sharp blade.

Ganin swung his fist just at the moment that Carter drove the blade into the Russian's throat, then pulled with every ounce of his waning strength to the left.

A huge gush of bright red arterial blood spurted out of Ganin's neck. He clutched at his throat, and before he fell back, dead, he looked down at Carter, his nostrils flared.

You have won, my friend, he seemed to say. *Despite my best, you have won.*

Carter lay back in the snow, his eyes closed, his world spinning around. Ganin had been good. The very best he had ever gone up against. But it still was incredible to him to think that Kobelev could have survived the impact on the train so long ago. He had watched the bridge hit the Russian in the back of the head. He had seen Kobelev's body fall off the train, bounce off the rocks below, and then be swept away in the river.

But the man had survived. His power was awesome.

Another vision came to Carter, this one more recent—Kobelev hanging out the side of the helicopter as it went down.

Was it possible? Had Kobelev survived again?

Carter opened his eyes, and the shock of what he saw was nearly physical. Kobelev, blood seeping from a wound in his chest, a gash at his forehead, and a maniacal look in his eyes, stood there. He held an American made Thompson submachine gun in his hands, pointed at Carter, and his hands were shaking so badly the weapon was likely to go off at any moment.

"Yes, it's me," the Russian screamed. He laughed.

Carter held very still. His Luger was out of reach in his coat pocket, and his stiletto was half a foot away from his left hand, lying blade up in the bloody snow.

"This time you won't get away from me," Kobelev said. "This will be for my daughter, Tatiana, and most of all for Istanbul."

The Thompson's safety was off. Carter could see it from where he lay. Kobelev's finger was curled around the trigger. One squeeze and it would be impossible to miss. There would be no chance of survival.

"But first you're going to beg," Kobelev said softly. He calmly moved the Thompson a little lower, and squeezed off one shot.

The bullet tore into Carter's left thigh, just below his groin, the force of the impact nearly pulling his hip out of joint, the pain so intense it boiled up into his gut, and constricted his chest, making it difficult to breathe.

''You're going to know real pain,'' Kobelev shouted. He squeezed off another shot, this one smashing into Carter's right foot, breaking his ankle.

''What do you want?'' Carter screamed. His only chance now was his stiletto.

Kobelev laughed again, spittle drooling down the sides of his mouth. ''You're going to beg, Carter,'' he cried. ''You're going to beg me to kill you. To put a sweet bullet into your brain.''

He fired a third time, this bullet grazing Carter's left side, breaking at least one rib.

''No,'' Carter shouted. ''Please!''

Kobelev's eyes were wide; his madness was like a huge electrical charge energizing him. He danced backward a foot or so. ''Crawl to me, Carter! I want you to crawl to me! I demand it. You will kiss my boots, and then I will end it, mercifully, with a bullet in the back of your head. Now! Crawl!''

He fired off a short burst inches from Carter's head.

''Crawl!''

It was all the opening Carter needed.

''I don't know if I can move,'' he cried.

Kobelev fired another short burst very close to Carter's head. ''Move! Now!''

With all of his strength Carter managed to roll over, his hands outstretched, clutching the snow as if he were trying to pull himself forward. He found the stiletto, the blade slicing into his left hand, but then Kobelev was directly over him, the barrel of the Thompson pressed against the base of Carter's skull.

''Beg me for death, and I will kill you now,'' Kobelev shouted.

Carter had the handle of the stiletto. ''No,'' he cried weakly, pushing himself half up, and then he slumped facedown in the snow as if he had fainted, but every muscle in his body was bunched up, ready to strike like a coiled spring.

"Beg it of me!" Kobelev screamed. "Beg!"

The barrel of the Thompson moved away, and Kobelev bent down, grabbed Carter's shoulder and pulled him over.

At that moment, Carter rose up and drove the stiletto to its hilt in Kobelev's groin.

The Russian reared back, bellowing in rage and pain. Carter scrambled after him, his left leg useless.

Kobelev could not bring the Thompson around to fire at Carter, but he used the heavy weapon as a club, smashing at Carter's back and head, fighting like the totally insane monster he had become, screaming at the top of his lungs in Russian.

Carter's fingers sought and found Kobelev's throat, and he squeezed with everything he had left, the Russian's eyes bulging as he thrashed around.

It could not last much longer, Carter knew. His own wounds were too extensive. He didn't have much strength now. Once again his world was starting to go gray and his concentration was reduced to his grip on the Russian's throat. Again a vision of Sigourney's body in the ashes of the cabin swam into his mind's eye. All of it, all of the pain and suffering and killing had been simply to flush out Carter. Nothing more than a vendetta.

There would be others after Kobelev and Ganin. But never could there be such a combination of evil genius and dark purpose.

Kobelev's body gave a mighty shudder, and then lay still. But for a long time afterwards Carter kept squeezing. This time he must make sure. This time there would be no doubts . . .

DON'T MISS THE NEXT NEW
NICK CARTER SPY THRILLER

THE BERLIN TARGET

Bending low, Carter duck walked the width of two beach houses and dropped into the rear garden of the only one with lights glowing.

The air was sweet with blooming flowers and buzzing with insects. The only other sound as he wound his way through scrub and low citrus trees was a radio playing something maudlin from one of the nearby rooms.

He headed in that direction and carefully brought his eyes up over the window ledge.

He was just in time. It was the bedroom of the *dacha*, and Anna was just emerging from the bathroom, stark naked. He watched her pull on a pair of sheer panties and encase her voluptuous breasts in a lacy, very unproletariat bra.

Over that went a tight sweater and slim skirt, an outfit that should have made the hair on the back of his neck and inner thighs tingle.

It didn't.

It made the scar across his chest itch and ache.

He scanned the room. A half-packed suitcase lay open on the bed. Two closed cases sat by the door. He couldn't see a phone, and there was no sign of a weapon.

Anna went to work on her dark hair, and Carter took a turn around the whole house. He ended up back at the sliding glass doors that led from the garden into a large sitting room.

The room and its decor was about as far removed from the hovel where he and Ludmilla had spent the night as Washington was from Moscow.

The party elite and their favored people didn't suffer.

The room was done well, in soft tones, and the furniture was modern and expensive. Chrome-framed prints and antique tapestries somehow worked together on the walls. The prints were French Impressionist paintings and, strangely enough, were mostly Renoir nudes.

The sliding doors opened easily, and he moved into the room. He finally located the phone and cut the cord. When the intercom on the wall was jammed, he moved to a well-stocked portable bar.

It was foolish, he thought, but something deep inside him made him want to handle it this way.

He sloshed vodka into a glass, unholstered the Makarov, and sat down to wait.

It wasn't long. She glided into the room, still brushing her hair, and came up short with a gasp six feet from where he sat.

She was even more beautiful and arresting from the front than she had been from the rear. And, up close, the tight-fitting clothes left little to the imagination.

"You! How . . .?"

"Good evening, Anna," Carter said, saluting her with the glass and the long snout of the Makarov's silencer.

It hit her hard, but it took only seconds for her to regain composure.

She was a cool cookie, he thought, like ice, as he tossed her hair from her face and took in the pistol and wet suit at a glance. The hard, dark eyes finally settled on his. They spoke challenge, and he answered it.

"Submarine?" she growled.

"In the Black Sea? Of course not. This is your turf. That would be far too dangerous. But I did emerge from the sea like a nymph."

She started to turn toward the bedroom, her strong thighs moving steadily, lushly visible under the skirt. They stopped moving when Carter put a slug into the doorjamb two inches from her shoulder.

If she was unnerved when she turned back to face him, she didn't show it. But her mind was obviously working, and her eyes were darting from Carter to the glass doors.

"Go ahead," he said. "But I wouldn't advise it. Your guards aren't there. Mine are."

She shrugged, then moved to the bar. "I should have made sure you were dead in Berlin."

"Yes, you should have."

"You are a clever, dangerous, and resourceful man."

"Yes, I am."

She poured a drink and walked past him to the opposite sofa. She rolled her long legs under her like a cat. When she spoke again, she also purred like one.

"You've come for Boris."

Carter nodded. "Why go through all this to get what he knows? Why not just use a needle?"

"Two reasons," she replied in a bored voice, "and you should know both of them. We routinely, daily, take antidotes to combat truth chemicals . . . yours. Unfortunately, they also contradict our own drugs. There wasn't time to hospitalize Boris until the chemicals would work."

"And the second reason?"

"We were not positive that he had turned." She sipped her drink and smiled. The smile was far from warm and friendly, but it did fantastic things to the fine bones of her face. "We are now."

"*Touché*," Carter replied, smiling himself.

"Boris is a spineless jackass, but he works well in the West. He also has a genius for organization."

"An organization that you are now completely aware of."

"Perhaps." Her eyes came up, mirroring the vacant coldness of his own. "You managed somehow to get in here, but you'll never get out, not two of you. And, besides, I'm not so sure Boris will go with you . . . now."

"I think he will. You're very beautiful, Anna, but not beautiful enough to die for."

The door opened, slammed, and Boris Simonov emerged from the alcove and walked into the room behind Anna. He was tall and spare, with a weak chin. His dishwater-gray eyes grew wide with shock when he saw the tableau before him.

"Who . . ."

"Hello, Boris. Or I imagine I should call you Peter, since I've come to get you out."

"How did you . . ."

Anna slid off the sofa and slithered to his side. Possessively, she curled her arms around one of his.

"His name is Nicholas Carter," she said. "He's a one-man American assassination team, and he's probably come to kill you."

Simonov went even paler and shifted his eyes from Carter to the woman and back again.

"Let me give it to you straight, Boris," Carter growled, getting to his feet and making sure the barrel of the Makarov was trained solely on the woman. "They found out that we turned you. That's why you were called back. This 'wife' you were supposed to acquire was only meant to get what's in your head so that another deep-cover agent could go in and take up where you left off."

"Preposterous!" Anna said, and tugged harder, trying to keep him against her.

It didn't work. Simonov was already backing away from her, his face a chalky white and his body shaking in fright.

"It's true, Boris. Anna was supposed to get everything out of you she could, and then you were on your way back to Moscow. Where were you headed when you left here tonight, Boris?"

"Moscow," he stammered.

"And from there it was a gulag, at best. At the worst . . ." Carter shrugged, leaving Simonov to fill in the inevitable.

"It's true, isn't it?" the frightened man said, staring at the woman he had probably been making love to the past two nights. "Isn't it?"

Annas knew she'd been unmasked. The Killmaster could see it in her eyes.

Carter thought, wrongly, that she would go for him. Anna was too much the trained agent. Instead of Carter, she went for Simonov. If the Russians couldn't retain what he had accomplished in the West, then the Americans wouldn't have it either.

She was like a panther, fast and sharp. In a split second she had the narrow chain belt from her waist around Simonov's throat. Her hands were trained, skilled in killing.

Simonov was no match for her, and Carter couldn't get in a shot without hitting him. The belt became a garrote, and her knee in the small of his back was doing the rest of the work.

Carter had only seconds, and he used them.

It was useless to try and flank her. Everywhere the Killmaster approached, she turned Simonov's body to head him off.

Finally he gave up and plowed into both of them. His shoulder hit Simonov in the gut, driving the wind from him and slamming Anna into the wall.

The long barrel of the Makarov cracking across one of her wrists brought enough slack in the belt to allow Carter's fingers to get between it and the man's neck.

When Carter pulled it away, Simonov fell to the floor gagging. Anna recovered instantly, even though it was obvious that her right wrist was broken. With the fingers of her left hand curled, she went for Carter's throat.

—From THE BERLIN TARGET
A New Nick Carter Spy Thriller
From Charter in February 1986

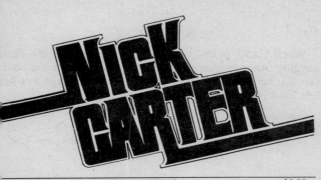

Bestselling Thrillers—
action-packed for a great read